Be Careful What You Wish For

Author: Laura J. Wellington

WORDS MATTER
P U B L I S H I N G
OUR WORDS CHANGE THE WORLD

© 2020 by Laura J. Wellington. All rights reserved.

Words Matter Publishing
P.O. Box 531
Salem, Il 62881
www.wordsmatterpublishing.com

ISBN: 978-1-949809-93-0

Library of Congress Catalog Card Number: 2020946549

Dedication

For Dean R. Wellington. I'm smiling.

Table Of Contents

Prologue

I must confess that it was never my aspiration to become a fiction author or write this book. But it seems we have moved to a place where too many of us have abandoned the notion that soul-binding love exists, the kind between two people that breaks barriers and crosses planes. Otherworldly in the making. So unfortunate. So mistaken.

I'm here to change such thinking as I've known this type of love. It overtakes you upon meeting and refuses to die, even when the heart stops beating. It is rare but it is real. To reject this is to deny yourself the chance of ever experiencing it. So many do, forsaking the very essence of what makes our time here on earth worth living.

"Be Careful What You Wish For" redefines romance beyond common definition. Passionate and compelling, it explains why parted souls are so driven to find each other again. And although Rick and Evie's story is largely fiction, the never-ending love in which it was written ISN'T. As I said, I've lived it.

Chapter 1

The Inspection

As I carefully arranged the store-bought cookies on the antique plate I recently purchased at my favorite thrift shop, my attention quickly turned to the tea kettle. Water spit from the spout as if to demand that I no longer ignore it. Turning off the burner, I poured the boiling liquid into a beautifully crafted china pot in which cinnamon-apple tea bags lay.

My gosh, I hope she doesn't realize that these cookies are from Dollar General, I thought to myself.

I cringed at the very idea, knowing full well that my blunder to plan my morning out better would cause me to fail as "ultimate hostess."

"Oh, well, HGTV worthy, I am not."

No sooner had those words fallen from my lips when a knock came from the door. My body stiffened in anticipation of meeting the woman who stood on the other side. Caught between feelings of excitement and nervousness, I found my feet again. A quick prayer accompanied me into the foyer. "I hope I know what I am doing," I said to myself. Then grabbing the doorknob, I pulled.

"Evie Remington?" the woman inquired.

"Yes," I responded eagerly with a large grin planted on my face.

"Very nice to meet you. My name is Debra Torre. I'm here to go over all of the details of your application with you and to inspect your home." She handed me her card.

"Very nice to meet you too," I replied, taking the card from her hand and holding the door wide open for her to make her way inside. The task wasn't a small one given the boot she was lugging around on her right leg.

Slowly, she made it over to the kitchen table. Then pulling out a chair to sit, she lowered herself into it. A heavy sigh of relief followed, one which made me feel even worse about the store-bought cookies.

"Dear God," I said to myself as I brought the plate, pot, and two teacups over to the table. Taking a seat opposite her, I began to pour the dark liquid into both cups. When doing so, I asked Debra the obvious question—"What happened to your foot?"

She explained the story of how the fire alarm had suddenly gone off in her house. Startled, her rashness caused her to trip down the stairs in order to usher her children to safety. I imagined the scenario as she described it. "Unfortunately, this means that I will need to come back to inspect your second floor," she stated as she pulled a rather fat folder from her case.

"No worries," I said. "Cookie?"

"That's very kind of you," she replied, pulling a cookie from the edge of the plate and popping it into her mouth. "Mmmm. Just what I needed." She took a second one and placed it on the saucer next to her teacup. "These are great!"

Little did she know that her pleased reaction was just what I needed to put my racing heart to rest. My concerns quieted down too, leaving me to get to know this woman beyond the pivotal role she would be playing in the life-changing event I was about to embark upon. I liked her and found myself grateful that "she" was the one whom the agency had arranged to lead me down this new path I'd chosen to travel.

"It's better if we take this slow," Debra began. "Not good to speed the process...for anyone."

I nodded, yielding to Debra's wisdom.

Grabbing a pen and pad of paper from inside her bag, Debra began to scribble some notes. Then shifting her glance back towards me, she proceeded to ask a variety of questions based upon the information that I had already given at the recent open house. Little effort was needed to answer any one of them. They all seemed rather generic and uninteresting until the moment Debra began inquiring about what was indisputably the most painful period in my life—the tragic passing of my husband, Rick.

"What do you believe is your greatest strength?" Debra questioned.

"Resilience," I replied, without hesitation. A host of memories came flooding back as I said it.

Reflected in my face, Debra sat, anticipating a larger explanation to follow. Silence permeated the room. When she realized none was forthcoming, she pressed further, unleashing a wave of tears and tales that proved impossible to contain...even years later. "Tell me, dear," I could hear her say in an effort to coax me from my thoughts.

I was reminded of how strangers could uncover hidden vulnerabilities and anguish better than the familiar at times. This was one of those times.

My head began to ache. No longer able to suppress my thoughts, I started to speak. I left nothing to the imagination.

Chapter 2

The Meeting

Dropping my phone back into my pocket, I re-entered the building with a container full of Chinese broccoli, a buttered bagel and a recognizably disgruntled demeanor. I was fed up...fed up with Steven and his unrelenting self-indulgent personality. I was tiring of him, no longer satisfied with the routine that had slowly become our norm.

Where had the spark gone? I thought to myself as I placed the brown bag on my desk and fished for a fork in my side drawer. That answer was far from a mystery. Alcohol and the demands of an overbearing father seemed to be sucking the life out of my relationship with Steven. The realities of the family business were taking its toll and I became more convinced than ever that my days with Steven were numbered. His only saving grace for a while now had been my fondness for his mother. We had grown close when away from the men and I really didn't want to hurt her. But even that argument was starting to wane.

"I guess I will go to the restaurant opening myself," I uttered, knowing, full well, that most of my co-workers had already been planning to attend anyway. It would be a fun night regardless of Steven's absence. "Maybe even more fun," I burst out loud, not realizing how angry I actually was until then.

I grabbed the bagel and took a huge bite. The mouthful of carbs seemed to calm my temper, leaving me to tackle the rest of my day in a better frame of mind. *Why waste my time with a bad attitude and an ungrateful man,* I thought to myself. The rest of the afternoon flew by. By six o'clock, I had completed all of my assignments and prepared everything to easily dive back into my work the following morning.

"Time to join the rest of the office," I said to myself as I retrieved my coat from the nearby closet and waved "good-bye" to my boss. Caught on the phone, he motioned his disappointment in not being able to join us in our fun. I mimed a crying expression then gathered my things and left. Refreshed, by the ten-minute walk it took to get to O'Shaughnessy's, I arrived in really good spirits, eager to find my other co-workers.

The crowded doorway led to a highly populated bar area. I pushed my way through, eventually spotting a face that I knew standing next to a circular table just a few feet away. As I carved a path towards her—constructed of polite gestures and proper apologies—I could feel the back of my sweater tug, one time then another. I turned in horror, fully expecting to face the blundering actions of a drunken degenerate barely capable of understanding exactly what he had done nor how costly the garment had, unmistakably, been.

"One full paycheck," I mumbled under my breath. No sooner had I said it when my eyes locked on the most perfect grin that I had ever seen. A sucker for smiles, *his* was unusually captivating. It widened as he unhooked his cuff from my sweater.

"I am so sorry," he said, realizing the giant hole that his clumsiness had left behind. "Please allow me to pay for the damage...or replace the sweater altogether."

I'm not sure if it was my pride or the genuine upset I saw in this man's piercing blue eyes that compelled me to refuse his offer. I did exactly that, though, then continued on my original path, closing in on my co-workers who were still waiting for me. I greeted everyone as cheerily as possible while doing my best to act unfazed by the blaring hole in the top half of my outfit. Looking over my shoulder in an effort to lessen the obviousness of the unfortunate collision, I wove one thread underneath another and made a knot. *It would do for now,* I thought to myself then returned my attention to the rest. Seconds later, I could feel the presence of someone standing directly behind me. It was the same man who had torn my sweater. This time our meeting was no accident.

He waited—patiently hoping that I might turn my eyes his way before too long. I could feel his gaze resting upon me. Incapable of avoiding him any longer, I shifted my body in the direction of his and waited for him to do something.

"Can I, at least, buy you a beer?" he asked, discontent with allowing the issue to pass without making some amends.

"You can," I replied, happily allowing the handsome stranger to make things right and even happier to have the chance to get to know him.

No girl ever prayed so hard that the "luck of the Irish" would continue to intervene that evening. I felt oddly attracted to this man from the onset—a reaction quite foreign to me. I normally wasn't so forcefully drawn to any man, despite good looks or the usual characteristics that made someone attractive to most. My type could only be described as "quirky" and this particular individual seemed anything but. And yet, I found myself studying his every feature, indulging fully in the attraction I felt towards him while weighing all of the possibilities that could arise from our chance meeting.

He returned carrying two Guinnesses and, carefully, handed me one.

"The last thing I need to do now is pour a drink on you," he remarked.

"Murphy Lives," I chuckled. It seemed to place all nervousness aside and invite the type of banter more akin to old friendships than sudden acquaintances. With each hour that passed, our initial comfort continued to evolve. We talked about everything—life, work, family, schooling, relationships, dreams. I even told him about Steven, a revelation that did little to dissuade him. Like me, he was completely absorbed and he wasn't about to let something as trivial as a worn-out relationship get in his way. Doing all that I could to keep my composure, I began to suspect that I might have unknowingly walked head-first (or should I say "back" first) into my destiny that night.

Time will tell, I thought to myself as I scribbled down my number using the pen he offered me which bore his family name—"Remington." I would, eventually, learn the power the Remingtons wielded just as I would realize both the responsibility and burden adopting such a name held.

Disappointed by the howling that nearly always accompanies "last call," I agreed to let this handsome "new man in my life" walk me to my car. Once there, I struggled to find my keys, so hidden were they within the crevices of my handbag and anxious was I about the dawning of reality in the midst of such a heavenly evening.

"I look forward to seeing you again, Evie," I heard him say.

"I do too, Rick," I replied, dreading my departure and hoping that tomorrow would come quickly.

He pulled me close to him—an embrace that I'd remember for a lifetime. Then removing my keys from my hand, he unlocked the car door, placed me inside, and asked me to text him when I arrived home.

His genteel manner floored me, leaving me to grapple with any response at all. "I will," I answered, feeling my heart skip a beat as I did. Removing his hand from the door handle, he gave me a "thumbs up" in response then watched as I backed out of the space, nearly hitting him in the process. Leaping out of the way, he gave me a "thumbs up" again, laughing as he positioned himself a few extra feet from where my car almost killed him.

It was at that exact instant that I fell in love.

Chapter 3

The Dance

By two o'clock the next day, I began to second-guess myself about the night before, including the character of the man I'd met. I had yet to hear from him. And even though he told me that he'd be teaching at his alma mater hours away, I was still convinced that he would have called by now. "Obviously, you were wrong," I said to myself in a disappointed tone. My heart sank at the thought that Rick might truly never call at all.

I began to feel stupid—naive even. So many times my friends had told me that men like Rick Remington just didn't exist. "Only in the movies," they'd insist, dashing my dreams and any hope I had left in me. Regardless, I refused to believe them...up till now, that is. Disheartened and annoyed by my childish resistance, I no longer felt so certain or compelled to fight the consensus.

A few hours later, I began to revisit my relationship with Steven in my head. "Maybe, it wasn't so bad after all? Maybe, I was expecting too much from him? It wasn't as if everyone who met Steven didn't love him," I said to myself.

"Except you," another small voice inside me argued.

"Oh, shut up," I retorted, upset that my attempt at denial was failing so profoundly. The internal dialogue nearly caused me to miss the ringing of my cell phone. Hearing it suddenly, I grabbed it and frantically pounded on the little green icon.

"Evie," I heard him say. "It's Rick."

My heart leaped, forgiving me for my temporary insanity regarding Steven's suitability and our improbable future in light of Rick's phone call.

"Hi Rick," I replied, as calmly as I was capable of doing under the circumstances. *Thank God he couldn't see me*, I thought to myself. *He'd think I was a lunatic.*

"Listen," he continued. "I've decided to return home tonight as opposed to tomorrow morning. I'd like to get together this evening if possible. I understand that it's short notice but I wanted to ask if you would like to have dinner with me? I know a great place. It's quiet...has terrific food, music and even a fireplace. It would be late."

It took everything that I had to contain myself. "Late's no problem," I responded.

"Great," he said. "I will text you the address and meet you outside at 9 pm. If anything changes, let me know and I will do the same. Oh, and Evie," he hesitated. "You've been on my mind all day."

He hung up quickly before I even had the chance to respond. "You've been on my mind too," I replied softly.

The rest of the afternoon went by like a blur. By eight-thirty, I had tried on countless outfits and played out all types of scenarios in my head, hoping to figure out what the night would hold before it even happened. The futility of this was apparent but I just couldn't help myself.

Checking my face in the bathroom mirror once again, I collected my things and slammed the door behind me. I was heading back to Fort Lee, the same town where I had first met Rick the night before. "I'm beginning to really like Fort Lee," I said to myself.

Already a bit dark, I was grateful that I had my GPS to direct me. I never was particularly good at navigating on my own, especially when it came to busy towns as unfamiliar as this one. Thirty minutes later, the monotone voice I'd become accustomed to announced that I had arrived, leaving me confused as I surveyed the two-story residence standing in front. It was beautiful, crafted in brick and stone. And there seemed to be a door left open on the second floor.

I parked then called Rick from my car. He answered while walking outside through that same doorway. His casual sweatpants, striped button-down shirt, and plaid socks made him look more "clown" than "desirable bachelor," bringing more sense to my attraction for him. *He obviously has a few quirks after all,* I thought to myself as I waited to hear his voice.

"Hi, Evie," Rick said, looking straight at me as he did. A big grin covered his face.

"Hi, Rick," I replied, meeting his grin with one of my own.

"Coming up?" he continued.

"I don't know," I answered, chastising myself for overlooking the one possibility in the list of scenarios I had contemplated. "Is this your apartment?"

"It is," he replied. Then realizing my reluctance, he continued, "I promise, Evie...I will be a complete gentleman."

My thoughts were darting all over, weighing out whether or

not I should trust him. *Well, so far so good and you know he has a fireplace. You can always hit him over the head with the poker*, I rationalized. Pulling the keys from the ignition, I opened the car door, then shut it behind me.

When I reached the top of the stairs, Rick gave me an enormous hug, lifting me right off of my feet. He ushered me inside and pointed in the direction of his kitchen table. A vase filled with a dozen multicolored roses sat.

"Those are for you," he said. "See...had you not come in, I couldn't have given them to you."

"They're beautiful," I replied, spotting a gray marble fireplace over his shoulder. "Thank you, Rick." My mind now at peace, I walked over to the vase, plucked a rose from the center and breathed. The smell was intoxicating, a sign of the night ahead.

"You are very welcome, Evie," he answered. "How could I not? They reminded me of you. By the way," he continued. "Now, we are even."

Baffled by his comment, I plopped the rose back into the vase and walked closer to him. I was determined to fully understand what he meant in saying such a thing.

"Even?" I inquired.

"Yes, even," he responded. "I wrecked your sweater and you wrecked my car."

As I was no closer to knowing what he meant, I pressed the matter further, leading me to learn that he had experienced a car accident during his long trip home. Tired from the late night prior and a long day of teaching, he had fallen asleep at the wheel and ended up in a bank at the side of the road. No one was hurt. His car was another matter. "The damage was minor but expensive," he noted.

"It happened because I wanted to see you," he said. "So, yes. I believe we are now even. You might even owe me, but I'll let it slide," he flashed a devilish grin.

I shook my head while rolling my eyes. Then replied, "Has anyone ever told you that you are incorrigible?"

"You see that already," Rick laughed. "Yup, my mom." Then continuing, he said, "Has anyone ever told you that "cars and you" don't mix?"

"What?" I cried, playing along with his teasing, an astonished expression on my face.

"Yes, first you nearly run me over...then you cause me to land in a ditch. I don't think you have good "car karma" if you ask me. Might be tough on a relationship." He winked when he said it. "Wine?" he continued.

"I think I need it," I answered, realizing just how much fun... and challenging...this man could be.

He picked up a glass from the counter, pulled a bottle of red from the refrigerator and poured. He handed it to me. Reaching back in the fridge, he grabbed an iced tea for himself.

"You're not having some?" I remarked.

"Nope," he replied. "I don't drink much, actually. I can't really. I have Crohn's disease. Bad for the system."

It was the second time that evening I had no idea what Rick meant. He would soon explain. I'd come to learn that Rick had been diagnosed with Crohn's disease as a junior in college. An autoimmune disorder, Rick remained in the care of Dr. Crohn's, its namesake, ever since.

"Staying on my medication and regulating my diet, I almost forget I have the disease. It won't shorten my life any, that I know," Rick continued to say.

Relief washed over me. I was glad to hear that the disease was easily managed for him and especially glad to know that it wouldn't shorten his life. I could feel myself liking him more and more. The notion of him "sticking around" was growing increasingly important, well-beyond the two days it warranted. I felt rattled by anything that could prevent this.

Returning back to the conversation, I teased, "I guess that makes you human. Any other surprises you want to drop on me?"

"Nodda one," he retorted. "Unless you have something against dating Jewish men."

Pivoting my foot towards the stairs, I strode over to the door then motioned my exit. The room fell silent. It provided the perfect backdrop for the following response, "I don't. I'm dating one right now. Steven's Jewish."

"Good to know," Rick said. "You got half of that statement right."

Rick's incorrigible nature would triumph again, as would his directness, intelligence, and romantic demeanor. He left me speechless.

"Make sure you take that foot out of your mouth before you eat," Rick chuckled, dipping a fork into one of the pots on the stove and placing the morsel on my tongue.

The taste was spicy...similar to the mood in the room, currently. Taking a cue from both, I closed my eyes, raised my chin, and dared him to kiss me. I could sense Rick moving closer——the warmth of his lips radiating near mine. Then, all of a sudden, he drew back.

"Nope. I promised to be a gentleman."

Moving over to the table, he picked up a plate and handed it to me. By this time, my eyes were wide open, amazed by his restraint yet wildly disappointed. I felt hungry for him but it was obvious that dinner was the only item on the menu that night. *Oh, well,* I thought. *He's doing what you asked him to do.* I wanted to kick myself. At the same time, I was grateful to learn that Rick was "a man of his word." Too many men weren't. I'd had enough of *those* in my life already.

Filling our plates, we took our food and drinks into the living room, set them near the fireplace, and sat on the floor, eating. It was our first meal together—the first of many to come. I liked that idea, immensely. I liked everything about Rick. I felt as if someone needed to pinch me to prove that I wasn't dreaming, but then again, if I was, I didn't want to wake up.

We spent the rest of the evening cuddled together, watching the logs burn down while our desire for each other heated up. Lightly stroking my hair, Rick drew me closer. His touch both excited and calmed me. Feeling uniquely vulnerable, he could have asked me for anything at that particular moment, and I would have said "Yes." And then he did...but it wasn't anything I could have ever imagined.

"How about we play Hangman," Rick stated.

Normally posed as a question between potential players, this time it didn't seem to be. Rick wanted to play Hangman. Why? I had no idea. "Hangman?" I mimicked him.

"Yes, Hangman," Rick continued. "Turn around and I will use your back as the surface. See if you can guess the phrase."

"Alright," I replied. *Any touch from Rick was welcomed,* I thought to myself.

Rick began writing letters with his fingertip. W...then H...A...T. I guessed the first word quickly—"What." The next six words took a bit longer—"are we going to do about...."

The final word, however, I deciphered right away—S...T...E...V...E...N. Then putting them all together, I mouthed, "What are we going to do about Steven?"

"Good question," Rick teased. "What ARE we going to do about Steven?"

I fell silent, not knowing what to say or what he wanted me to say. Turning my face towards him, I raised both eyebrows noting my confusion.

"You look confused," Rick commented. "Well, how about I unconfuse you, Evie?"

He continued. "I'd like to date you and see where this goes, but Steven needs to be out of the picture. I'm willing to give you until tomorrow night after I take you out again, but then that's it, Evie, or Saturday morning...I'm going sailing by myself!"

Contemplating the ultimatum Rick had just handed me through a game of Hangman, I didn't know whether to be pissed off or flattered. I chose flattered. Then thinking over my time with Steven, my answer couldn't have been easier. It was reflected in my current dinner companion and the apartment I was sitting in. I knew in my heart that Steven and I were done.

"That's the last time I play Hangman with you," I responded while shaking my head and smiling.

Wrapping his arms around me from behind and pulling me closer, he whispered gently into my ear, "Evie, I mean it."

I replied in an equally soft voice, "I know."

An hour later, I was in my car, heading home again. My thoughts swirling, my heart screaming, I could barely follow my GPS's commands, ultimately getting myself lost along the way. When I finally reached my front door, I began to calm down.

Reading the call log on my cell phone, I noted Steven's name three times. I knew I needed to ring him back but I had no idea what to say. The thought of babbling some sort of excuse seemed less than appealing and I certainly wasn't ready to have the deeper conversation our time together warranted. With both options lacking, I decided to wait until the morning to speak with him.

Then washing the makeup off of my face and pulling a T-shirt over my head, I jumped into bed and began reminiscing about the evening I had just spent with Rick. I felt "lucky" and also tired. *No one dare pinch me*, I thought to myself as I closed my eyes. *No one at all.* With that, I drifted to sleep.

When I woke the next morning, I was exhausted. "Coffee," I cried, as I dragged me and my cell phone to the kitchen. I waved to my roommate on the way. Picking up the bag of blueberry grounds on the counter, I dumped two heaping tablespoons into the filter basket, added little water, then switched it on. *Strong was the word of the day*, I thought to myself. *No, "break-up" was the word of the day.* I knew I couldn't put it off any longer.

A deep sigh accompanied my dialing of Steven's number. After four rings, his voicemail picked up. Relieved, I spoke. "Steven. It's Evie. Call me when you have a few minutes. We need to talk."

"What happened then?" Debra asked, completely engrossed by every detail.

"I met Rick for dinner later that evening," I replied. "It was all very romantic, from the moment he scooped me up into his arms to the moment we parted. The wind and the rain were blowing so fiercely while we stood in the doorway kissing that he turned his back against them in hopes of keeping me dry. He made me feel so safe and cared for...that night and every one after that. Truthfully, Debra, I'd never met anyone like him."

"That, I believe," said Debra. "Sounds like a very special man. And what happened to Steven?"

"I traded Steven in for a pair of matching docksiders, the nickname "Snuggle Bunny," and an intoxicatingly sensual first kiss," I replied, vividly recalling all three.

Debra shifted in her seat. Her pained foot was becoming increasingly uncomfortable. That said, she wasn't about to get up and miss the rest of the story. She teased, "Girl...don't hold back on me now. I need to hear more about that kiss!"

I shook my head "No," determined to keep such a meaningful moment between Rick and me "sacred." It wasn't the intimate nature of it that compelled me to do so, rather the monumental one. Some moments between a man and a woman just shouldn't be shared with others, I believe, out of respect for the significance in which they represent...in our case, a very special beginning.

Understanding fully, Debra acquiesced. Then taking the second cookie from her saucer, she popped it into her mouth just as effortlessly as she had the first. Her mind was churning as her leg was throbbing. She rubbed it, took a sip of lukewarm tea, and waited, knowing fully that nothing in the world could make my words come fast enough. *Her foot would just have to cooperate,* she thought to herself.

"Worse case, I may just have to cut it off," she chuckled, sharing her thoughts with me.

I joined her in her humor as I pointed towards the knife block resting on the counter. Then winking smartly, I continued.

Chapter 4

The Courtship

From that day forward, Rick and I lived as if we were attached at the hip. We spent almost every waking moment together. Combining our lives seemed as effortless as combining our hearts. It all felt completely natural—holding his hand while driving in his sleek white 911 Targa, watching his face light up when he discovered a new gadget to entertain him, hearing his persistent attempts to sing alongside his favorite artists, even though we both knew he was completely tone-deaf. He made me laugh every time he tried.

As things progressed, it got to the point where I began to feel lost without him. Maybe that sounds a bit "needy" but the truth is, I did need Rick. We shared the kind of attachment I had been longing for my entire life and frankly, it felt good.

He was "my person" and it was evident that he felt the same about me. I could see it in his actions. He was tender, considerate, protective and enormously generous even though I never expected or asked him for anything. I wasn't a materialistic person. I think it was because of this that he enjoyed surprising me even more, including with fresh flowers every Friday evening. It came to the point where my tiny apartment began to look like a florist's shop.

My roommate seemed as delighted as me with every bouquet, quite enjoying the new splash of color in both our lives. She urged me to continue dating him, eager to see me happy while also relishing the significant change in our living arrangement. I was never around anymore and even though we missed each other, she loved the privacy and improved decor. Knowing that Rick and I were ecstatic too made it all the better.

Rick and I agreed. Neither of us could have been more excited or hopeful. A future filled with possibilities lay right in front of us. It seemed that we only needed to grab the dream to make it real. And so we did.

We spent our first few months together sailing in Connecticut. Those trips were something, I must say, filled with adventure and learning...including "how to sail" for me, anyway. I had never done it before. Now I was Rick's first-mate. I needed to know my way around his boat, a forty-six-foot beauty, as much as his life. I received a crash course in both.

With each and every lesson, we grew in understanding. We grew in affection. We sailed the sound. And we basked in each other's arms, with the occasional peanut butter and jelly sandwich split between us following long sessions of rampant love-making. The boat provided plenty of uninterrupted opportunities to do so. I adored being with him, satiating our appetites in ways only young love invites. Many weekends, we wouldn't even leave the dock, so wrapped up would we become in these moments.

Lying in his arms, naked and relishing the aftermath of one such occasion, Rick lured me into a conversation. He wanted to know my greatest fear.

"You mean, besides losing you?" I replied, only half kidding.

"Evie, you're never going to lose me," Rick answered. "First off, nothing is ever going to happen to me and second, I'm never going to leave you. So, what else frightens you?" he continued.

Thinking through that question further, I found myself entangled in a dilemma. Rick had stumbled upon a topic I rarely discussed with anyone—as my "sanity" could be called into question given my answer. My silence made Rick even more determined. He wasn't about to let it go, not unlike the first time we met and he followed me around the room due to my torn sweater.

"Evie," he spoke. "What's going on in that beautiful mind of yours?" Then nudging me back to my senses, he kissed my forehead and patiently awaited my response.

I sighed. Knowing that I needed to be forthright with Rick in order for us to work, I gathered my thoughts. Shifting my eyes back towards his, I began telling Rick a story about a time when I was a little girl.

"I had been sleeping soundly in my bed like every other night when I was awakened by a figure in my room quite suddenly. I could only see the outline, but I could feel the figure staring at me from the right side of my bed. Horrified, I went to scream but I couldn't. Nothing came out.

Realizing my absolute terror, this figure—I believe he was a man—immediately began communicating with me, but not through conventional means. I never even heard his voice. He spoke his thoughts through *here*." In circular motions, I began rubbing the center of my upper chest, indicating to Rick exactly where I had remembered. I then continued.

"The figure told me that he had no plans for malice, that he was simply there to "check on me," nothing more. He urged me not to be frightened, then told me that he would be back again. For now, however, I was to remember that he was watching over me and would help me whenever he thought I needed it or asked it of him. His involvement in my life would never cease."

An uncanny relationship abruptly surfaced between us upon realizing just how deeply this being, or spirit, cared for me. I'd never experienced anything like this before. Then, suddenly, he vanished, immediately releasing me from my temporary paralysis and compelling me to hop out of my bed and scramble for the light. "To this day, I can recall all of it, including how terrified I felt." I fell quiet again, nervous as to what Rick's response to my story might be. Then it came.

"Wow, Evie," he said. "Are you sure it wasn't a night terror?"

I replied sullenly, "That's exactly why I don't tell anybody. They either think I'm crazy or think I'm dreaming. But I'm not and I wasn't. I've felt him around since. I never even told my parents about it although I did have a subtle conversation with my father once regarding deceased relatives on his side of the proverbial tree. My sense was that this figure originated there. I concluded from what my father told me that the spirit, for lack of an absolute, was probably my great-grandfather, Tom."

"You did?" Rick replied.

"Yes, given how my dad described him," I answered.

"Hmmm," Rick continued. "Very interesting. Then let me ask you," Rick continued. "Is Great-Grandpa Tom here now?"

I knew Rick was teasing but I felt inordinately sensitive anyway. "No," I snapped, turning my back to him, insulted and annoyed.

"Evie," he stroked my hair. "I'm only playing with you. I also believe you," he continued.

"You do?" I asked.

"Yes, I do," he reassured me. "Besides, you needn't worry about it because when I solve my biggest fear, yours will be solved too."

I turned back around and asked, "What do you mean? What's your biggest fear?"

"Dying," Rick replied. "I don't want to die. Unfortunately, no one seems to have figured out how to stop that from happening yet. I've decided to make it my life's mission...once I'm tired of running the new company I want to launch, that is."

"*Curing dying* is on your agenda?" I remarked.

"Yup," he responded with a smirk, "especially now that I have so much to live for, Evie."

He carefully gauged my reaction to his comment, then kissed me lovingly on the lips as if to re-emphasize just how serious he was. I pulled him closer to me, wrapping myself further in his arms and holding tight. Then thinking through all that we had just shared, I realized that there was one outstanding question that remained. I blurted out, "What new company?"—indicating my absolute ignorance of his newest plan for our lives.

"The one you are going to help me build," he replied, lowering his head to the pillow while yawning deeply. "Let's talk about it further tomorrow. Your ghost tale has knocked me out plus we have a lot of shopping to do in the morning."

"We do?" I replied.

"Yes, we do," he said. "I want to introduce you to my favorite store, North Cove Outfitters. The company I help my dad out with sells a lot of product to them, hunting scents among other things. Because of this, I know the owners. I go there regularly, even during off hours. They'll open the store for me when I ask them to.

I've asked them "to" tomorrow. Expect to be lavished with a ton of new clothing and anything else that you want. You will be amazed by the extent of their inventory. They do a good job, I must say. You'll see tomorrow." With that, he covered me with a blanket as well as himself, blew out the candle, then whispered, "Good night, Snuggle Bunny. I love you."

"I love you, too, you crazy man," I answered, thinking about the day ahead, elated by Rick's surprise. *He never fails to amaze me,* I thought to myself.

With that, we both drifted off to sleep.

Chapter 5

The Family

The following Wednesday, Rick rang me at work. After learning that he had wanted to launch his own software firm just days prior, I found myself anxiously awaiting his father's reaction to the news. Rick told me that he was going to break it to him that day over lunch.

"Evie," Rick called out. "We've been summoned."

"Summoned?" I inquired, not having any idea what Rick meant.

"Yes, summoned," he continued. "I told Pop about the plans you and I discussed and then, of course, I told him about you. He's good with the plans but before he gives us his blessing on them, he wants to meet you. He's arranging a family get-together at the house on Saturday night. Everyone will be there. Are you ready for this?"

I didn't know what to say. What could I say except yes? Throwing the ball back into his court, I answered Rick. "I'm not quite sure but I'm ready to find out. Are you?"

"Evie," Rick replied. "If I wasn't, Dad wouldn't be summoning us."

By the time Saturday rolled around, my stomach felt like it had tied itself into a million little knots despite all of Rick's reassuring. "My dad will love you," he exclaimed. "And if you get nervous, just remember that you're speaking to Barry Liebowitz, not Baron Remington."

"I guess that's true," I said to myself, revisiting the story once again that transformed the Leibowitz family into the Remingtons. I found it amazing that Rick's father would assume a whole new identity and get away with it so that he might earn a living as an engineer during World War II. No doubt, his youth played a role in this decision as did the desperate times he encountered. Jews were not valued in any regard back then. Many were murdered in the camps. Others suffered. Some hid. To have the moxie to escape all this...change his name, re-cast the die, and alter his fate and future? The notion awed me. I admired his tenacity and cleverness. That said, my admiration didn't mean that he was going to like me.

When we arrived at the house in New Canaan, Connecticut, my jaw dropped open. It was a castle or so it seemed. I could hardly believe my eyes. "Oh my gosh," I screeched.

"Now, don't get nervous, Evie," Rick replied. "It's just a house."

"Maybe to you," I said. "But I hardly think the rest of the world would term this gigantic place "a house." A palatial estate or manor, maybe? But a house? No. Never." I continued to shake my head from right to left, overwhelmed with the opulence I was seeing in relation to the humbleness of the man seated next to me in the car. *He certainly adopted the digs to go along with the name,* I thought to myself.

"I heard that," Rick replied as if to convey that he could read my thoughts.

I rolled my eyes, then sighed, "Ahhh, Rick." He knew exactly what I meant....*incorrigible!*

Looking rather pleased with himself, he walked over to my door and opened it, all the while saying, "You might be right. Let's go inside anyway."

He took my hand into his and guided me up the stone stairway. Feeling extremely nervous now, I was additionally grateful for the warmth of his clutch. With each step, I grew more intimidated. Then taking a deep breath, I followed him inside.

"'Hey, Spencer!" Rick yelled as a very young child whizzed past us on a scooter. "Where's Pop?"

The little boy pointed upstairs while continuing to push himself as quickly as he could. We were soon joined by two other children, a bit older but not by much. The little girl ran over to Rick and jumped into his arms. She gave him a big hug. Rick squeezed her back then began to tickle her, sending her into fits of delight. The clamor drew the rest of the family into the foyer.

Baron descended the stairs. "My boy," he cried. "Glad you could make it."

Rick placed the little girl on the ground then gave his father a big hug. Already feeling like a fish out of water—one that was on display no less—I waited for Rick to break free from his father's arms to introduce me. The few seconds that passed seemed like an eternity. Finally, Rick turned towards me and taking my hand into his own once again said, "Pop. Everyone. This is Evie."

Baron Remington fixed his eyes upon me. Then in his naturally charming manner stated, "Evie, my dear. Welcome to our home. We are so glad you could come." His smile was every inch Rick's or should I say Rick's was every inch Baron's. That's not all I would come to learn. Rick and Baron shared many of the same attributes, including one of being a big tease.

Lifting my arm and wrapping it around his own, Baron pretended to steal me away from Rick. He led me out of the foyer and towards the dining room, then stopped in front. Returning my arm to his son, he lowered his voice in a slight attempt to share a compliment he undoubtedly wanted the rest of the family to hear, "Fine choice, my boy!"

I was flattered and relieved. Knowing that I had passed muster with Baron put me at ease, allowing me the comfort I required to get to know the rest. Eight brothers and sisters as well as their spouses and kids were among them. Every one of Baron's ex-wives, except for Rick's own mother, was there too.

The family was indeed complex but peacefully choreographed. It was all very intriguing. Rick had already explained to me how dinner might go that night as well as the continued discourse between his two parents.

"You will never see the two of them in the same room together, I assure you, " he noted. *She'd have no part of Baron's charade,* is how she put it and what Rick told me. Needless to say, *theirs* wasn't a marriage or divorce made in heaven. Nonetheless, the rest of the family seemed to get along superbly.

"How about we go inside and eat," Baron stated. "Then afterward, boys, we will do our usual and play a bit of backgammon upstairs while Rachel gives Evie a tour of the house. Rachel was Rick's closest sister. They shared the same mother. It seemed to me, however, that that was the only thing Rachel wanted to share—not so keen was she on the idea that her big brother might be in love. She looked at me then Baron. Realizing that she wasn't going to get out of it, she forced an amiable smile.

Dinner didn't take long. Everyone was chatting merrily and with little restraint. I was struck by the looseness of the conversation especially as I had grown up in a home where everybody behaved in a more subdued manner. I found the difference refreshing and the Remingtons, enormously fun.

Rick leaned over to me, then quietly asked, "How are you doing, Snuggs?"

"I'm having a great time," I whispered back.

"Good," Rick said. "Would you mind if I went upstairs and played backgammon with the boys? It's sorta our thing."

"Not at all," I replied. "I'll hang out with your sister."

"Alright then," Rick said, pushing his chair away from the table. Then turning towards Rachel, he remarked, "She's all yours, Sis. Be good!" And with that, he was gone.

"My brother," Rachel remarked. "I guess he's frightened I'm going to scare you away." The sarcastic undertone of her comment further revealed the apparent upset my presence in Rick's life was causing her. I couldn't understand it. At the same time, I felt bad that it was happening. I continued to stay put at the table, patiently waiting until Rachel was ready to begin my tour.

"Well, come on then," she said, her face depicting her annoyance. "Let's start in the kitchen. You know what that is, right?"

Startled by her brash comment, I replied, "No idea whatsoever." I said it jokingly, trying to lighten the mood. It didn't work. I left it at that. Rachel was obviously angry with me for reasons I knew nothing about. As I normally chose the less confrontational route, I decided to do so this time too. I had already assumed that there might be a settling-in period required between us. I was fine with it.

What I wasn't fine with, however, was the sudden realization brought about by Rachel's candor denoting my lack of kitchen savvy. Cooking had never been my strong suit. *That needs to change*, I thought to myself. Lost in my head, I continued to keep silent.

Rachel did as well, except for sharing the names of each individual room that she showed me. They all came with fanciful titles for reasons that related to the decor held within, unique and inarguably stylish. An hour later, the tour was over.

The house was lovely, decorated in a variety of antiques and floral patterns. It seemed as "Connecticut" as Connecticut could be. The prior owner had been a major film star once-upon-a-time and you could see it in the lavish grounds and dramatic layout.

Standing back in the foyer, Rachel asked, "So what do you think of our humble abode?"

"It's incredible," I replied, marveling as I revisited every room in my head.

"Yes, it is," Rachel stated. Then, drawing a breath, she continued, "You know, he wants to marry you."

"What?" I responded, feeling completely caught off guard and a little bit strange. This wasn't a conversation I was prepared to have with Rick's sister, especially since Rick and I had yet to fully discuss it ourselves...or discuss it at all for that matter. Feeling a bit encroached upon, I digested what Rachel had just said to me as I waited to see if there was more forthcoming, admittedly.

"Rick wants to marry you. That's what this is all about, not some business he wants to launch. Rick told me so the night you guys met. He called me late that evening, really late, and told me that he had just met the woman of his dreams, the one he was going to marry. And apparently, that is so because he brought you here."

I was stunned, unable to find any words in which to respond. I just stood...thinking through an array of answers while waiting for the perfect one to enter my head.

"In any event, I thought you might like to know," Rachel continued. "So, if you are going to break his heart, do it before he asks you, will you please? Rick's been more like a father to me than an older brother. I am sure he filled you in on our childhood and how Pop left us when we were young. It was tough but Rick was always there for me and now he wants to be the same for you. So if you plan to hurt him, do it now. He is too good a person and he doesn't deserve to be hurt, not in the least."

Thinking back to conversations between me and Rick about his childhood, he had shared a few stories about when his father left but never once had he indicated how painful this reality had actually been for him or all of them it seems. I knew he didn't like to talk too much about it, beyond divulging that a heated argument over dinner one evening between his mother and father turned into a slap across the face. The next morning, his father was gone.

Rick wouldn't see him again until nine years later when Rick was eighteen years old. He called him two years before that, hoping to see Baron sooner, but his father told him to contact him again when he was old enough to drive. I thought Baron's reply was exceedingly cruel at the time that I had heard it but I knew enough about life "not to judge."

Now the pieces regarding Rachel's hesitance towards me began to fit together. She needed some reassurance that my feelings for Rick were genuine and lasting. "Rachel," I found my voice again. "I'm not going to break Rick's heart. I love him deeply."

"I hope you do," she said. "He means the world to me. He deserves to be happy and if you can do that for him then I'm on board."

"Thanks, Rachel," I replied, truly appreciating her feelings and directness.

"No problem," she said. "How about we find out what the boys are doing?"

"Sounds good to me," I agreed.

Following her up the stairs, Rachel threw open the door to her father's bedroom and announced, "Pop, we are done."

"Wonderful, my dear," he replied. Looking up and turning towards me, Baron asked, "What'd you think, Evie?"

"Lovely, Mr. Remington. Truly, truly, something to be proud of."

"We think so, my dear. Glad you do too as, I imagine, you will be spending a great deal of time here. And don't be so formal. Call me Baron."

"Thank you, Mr. Remington...I mean Baron," I replied, grateful for such a genial gesture.

My eyes caught Rick's, my expression indicating that all was fine and that I was enjoying myself. Rising from the bed, he announced, "Ok, everyone. Out! Pop wants to speak with Evie alone for a few minutes. Then we need to leave."

Dear God. Another surprise, I thought to myself. *My "resilience" was undoubtedly getting a work-out.* The trait had been the silver lining hidden within the sudden loss of my mother when I was ten. I'd always wished I'd come by it in another way. But regardless, my mom would have understood the value, especially today. She had always been a very resilient woman in her own right.

My father continued to remind me of our likeness, from the moment she passed away until the day he followed her a few years ago. "You could have been twins," he would say. As I grew up, I realized more and more what he meant. She and I were quite similar, my features altered slightly by my father's Italian heritage. Very slightly. Everything else was pure "Mom."

I saw it in the mirror every morning and in the veins in my hands as I worked through each afternoon. At night, I'd sit in my bed and study them, triggering thoughts of many difficult weeks of waiting. Altogether, however, it hadn't been much time. I'd place myself next to her, holding her hand and studying the thin blue lines protruding beneath her pale skin. I prayed...then prayed some more, nearly begging for her suffering to end. I never wanted to encounter such unfairness in my own life, nor for my kids to do so either when I had them. Convinced that the likeliness was remote, I took some comfort in the odds, albeit reminding myself that "fairness wasn't guaranteed to any of us," as I did.

My father raised me for many years thereafter on his own. Eventually, however, he would pass too, leaving me to keep company with fond memories of the both of them alongside a bunch of old photos. It was right about then that I also began to experience the occasional visit from two cardinals who I swore were sent by my mom and dad to remind me of their continued presence in my life and their love for me.

I had read somewhere that cardinals were good omens, long considered to be messengers from heaven. I never explored this further, wanting to believe it was true rather than merely folklore. It felt better this way.

Turning my attention back to my surroundings, my focus fell solely upon Baron. The room had since cleared, I came to realize. Embarrassed by the daze that I had unintentionally fallen into, I collected my wits and stood hoping to receive some sort of direction soon.

Baron rose from the bed, walked over to his closet and pulled out a velvet tray. Then returning to the spot he had left, he motioned for me to sit down next to him. Lifting the silk cover from it, there on display was a magnificent collection of jewelry, the extent of which could barely be described. Baron began to speak. "Evie," he said, "Rick has told me a lot about you. It seems that you have stolen his heart, which makes me very happy."

"Does anyone not know?" I cried out, thinking back to my conversation with Rachel minutes before. "A reality of being part of a large, close-knit family, I guess."

Baron agreed with a chuckle, then continued. "I'd like to give you a present. Pick one."

I couldn't believe my ears. I didn't know what to do, other than thank him, then politely decline. I had never been in this position before. It was oddly uncomfortable and flattering at the same time, neither of which placed me one iota closer to the proper response. I decided to go with my gut instinct. Before I had the chance to say anything, however, Baron stopped me, cutting my words off with some of his own. He'd already been a step ahead, insisting that he wouldn't take "No" for an answer.

Receiving my first taste of Baron's persuasive attitude, I began to understand just how he'd become the man he was today. "What else can you do?" I said to myself. "You have to pick one or you will insult him."

I chose a beautiful gold necklace with a simple black pearl centered between two yellow diamonds. It was the most exquisite piece of jewelry I had ever held, nevertheless, now owned. Opening the clasp, I put it around my neck and showed it off to him.

"Absolutely spectacular," Baron replied. "Great choice. You have a good eye, Evie, but then again, we already know that, now don't we dear?" Baron paused. "You are in love with my son."

"I am?" I teased, knowingly.

"Yes, you are, dear. I can see it in your eyes. And Rick is obviously in love with you too."

I smiled, unable to contain it.

"You must realize, Evie," Baron continued. "If you marry Rick, this is just the beginning."

"It is?" I replied, not certain where the conversation was now leading. Listening intently, I knew I was about to find out.

"Yes, my dear. It is. For starters, all of my daughters-in-law receive gifts of five thousand dollars a month each from me. The boys don't know about this so you would have to keep it quiet too, much like Jolene, Stacie, and I have done for years...and now, hopefully, you. There's also a bonus for each grandchild you give me. Consider it an incentive if you will. There is a lot more to discuss in this regard. We will get to it all as your relationship with my son unfolds, moves to a more permanent status. For now, I just wanted to broach this with you upfront...make you aware... and let you know that ultimately, Evie, everybody wins. And you will too. The girls receive extra spending money and my boys are kept happy."

Taking what Baron had just said to me all in, I couldn't believe my ears. *None of this was right nor what love was supposed to be,* I thought to myself. *I'd have no part of it.* Flabbergasted and insulted, I found myself stuck for a response. The last thing that I wanted to do was shoot myself in the foot but I also didn't want Baron to think that he was going to buy his way into controlling Rick's and my marriage or me, for that matter.

I was beginning to question what life among the Remingtons would actually be like. Maybe Estelle had been right in her decision to stay away. It made more sense to me now. That said, I loved Rick and wanted to spend the rest of my life with him, something I hoped he'd continue to want as well after tonight and the answer Baron was obviously waiting for.

Carefully, I considered my words. Then opening my mouth, I could feel my reply come tumbling out. "Baron," I said. "Thank you for such a generous offer, but I could never accept it. If you would like to give Rick five thousand dollars a month to help us get on our feet in our life together, I think that is a wonderful gesture but that is something between you and him, not you and me, as is the bonus money for our children."

Baron sat back in astonishment. His calculation had been off. He would now need to figure out a new strategy to remain at the helm of Rick's life, especially as Rick was the son being groomed to take over Baron's empire. Without control over him, Baron would lose control over everything.

Not used to being wrong, Baron picked up the tray of jewelry in dead silence and returned it to the closet. Then walking over to the door, he motioned for me to exit. I could hear Rick's laughter coming from the room where we had dined. Walking downstairs, I felt Baron's anger accompany my every step.

When Rick saw me, he jumped up and made his way across the room. I hugged him, desperately needing to feel some reassurance of his love for me. It didn't matter that he had no idea what had just occurred. I needed his arms around me.

"Oh, the two love birds," Baron remarked, standing in the doorway. "Rick, meet me in my office first thing on Monday. We need to go over a few particulars regarding this new venture of yours."

I felt like I was "put on notice" when he said it.

"Will do, Pop. We're heading out," Rick continued.

"Drive safe, my boy," Baron said. "And Evie, I look forward to seeing you again."

My heart sank. No doubt, Baron had just posed a challenge

to me right under his son's nose, not to mention everybody else's. I couldn't believe what was happening, but unwilling to give up without a fight, I replied, "Me too, Baron."

I fell silent for the first few minutes of our long drive home. As Rick seemed extremely pleased with the entire evening, I let him rattle on for a bit while I collected my thoughts. I didn't know whether to tell him about the conversation Baron and I had just had. Then again, I didn't know how I couldn't. I wasn't of the mind to keep secrets from Rick ever, but this was a doozy and I didn't know how he would react to learning about Baron's arrangement with his brothers' wives.

"I guess now's as good a time as any," I said to myself. And so I began. I told Rick everything. He sat quietly, half watching the road and half-listening to me. When my story was finally complete, he took a breath.

"Hmmm," he said. "Well, I'll be damned. I've never heard any of this before...not even a hint of it from Jolene or Stacie...nothing. Are you sure you got it right, Evie?" he questioned.

"Completely sure," I replied.

He seemed just as ruffled as I did when Baron approached me with this "once in a lifetime offer." When he finally digested it all, he stated, "Thanks, Evie, for letting me know. I'm going to talk with him about this tomorrow. I can't believe that he put you or me in such a crappy situation."

I breathed a huge sigh of relief. Grabbing Rick's hand, I said, "I'm really sorry that I had to tell you this, Rick. I just thought you should know."

"You were absolutely right to tell me. Oh, by the way," he continued. "What did you say?"

"Say about what?" I couldn't imagine what Rick was referring to. I had already remarked how I responded to Baron's distasteful gesture. *What was left?* I thought to myself.

"What did you say to Pop when he brought up the possibility of our getting married?"

"Oh that," I said jokingly. "I told him that I had been wishing for a proposal from you since the first day we met." I was hoping my wit would camouflage the truth hidden in that statement, but I wasn't quite sure that it had.

"I knew it," he teased. "But seriously, Evie. Have you thought about it?"

I didn't know what to say. I had thought about it, a lot but I wasn't quite sure that now was the right time to reveal this.

"Evie, come on. I genuinely want to know. Is that what you want?"

Realizing that I wasn't going to get out of the conversation I said, "That's exactly what I want, Rick. I want you. I want a life with you...to have your children...and to grow old together."

Rick smiled. "Be careful what you wish for, Evie. You just might get it," he answered, then continued, "I want that too."

Grabbing my hand, he squeezed it tightly. "One more thing," he went on. "Would you consider converting to Judaism? We could still celebrate Christmas and any other holiday that's important to you but, if we got married, I'd like our kids to be Jewish. The only way that could be is if you were."

"Where do I sign up?" I replied, having already realized from my life with Rick up to this point that this would probably be the case. I also happened to believe in the phrase "a house divided shall fall." Religion aside, the concept made sense to me now more than ever. Baron had seen to that. I didn't want to test those waters in any way. Rick's and my future together was just too important.

"Maybe we can talk to Saul about that when we have dinner with them on Thursday," Rick replied.

"Them?" I uttered. "Oh, yes...we are scheduled to have dinner with your mom and stepdad Thursday evening aren't we? I forgot. Will she be trying to bribe me too?" I chuckled at my joke, something I was known to do more times than not.

"Only with food," Rick laughed. "Mom loves to feed those she loves and she's going to love you."

"Hopefully not like your father," I teased.

"She's nothing like him," he reassured me.

And he was right. Estelle was extremely sincere and comfortable to be around. She also didn't mince words, a trait Rick obviously inherited from her. To that end, she had me calling her "Mom" even before our engagement was official.

Her husband, Saul, was equally as affable. Known as the life of the party wherever he went, some people referred to him as "The Mayor" because he knew just about everyone regardless of where the two found themselves. They could be visiting the Negev and, still, they'd run into someone they'd need to say hello to. I'd find that out later, first-hand, as it was a trip we would eventually take together. Needless to say, both were very easy to adore.

"So, Evie," Saul said. "Have you ever been to the Bergen Pac? I sit on the board there. It's a great place. Lots of wonderful shows. If you and Rick ever want to go, just let me or Mom know, and I'll get you tickets."

"Thanks, Saul," I replied, warmly. It was strange hearing Estelle referred to as "Mom" by Saul, equally as strange as when I said it, myself. Unlike with Steven, the idea of "gaining another mother" ran second to Rick's and my relationship. However, having Estelle thrown into the mix? I was elated to say the least. I found myself praying that my relationship with her might grow just as close as the one I'd shared with my own mom.

A flood of "missing" overwhelmed me unexpectedly. My mom had been on my mind a lot lately. It was hard to avoid given the onset and enormity of Rick's entire family. I began to selfishly wish that Rick's dream of "curing death" had ultimately been robbed of him years prior, that someone else had already figured the solution out. *She would be here today to see all of this if it had*, I thought. *Even meet Estelle. I bet they'd get along famously.*

I chuckled inside as I imagined these two women gabbing away about perfect moments inspired by their genius grandchildren, not unlike every other grandparent does. It would undoubtedly be something they had in common. The image delighted me. Then remembering that this would never occur, I could feel my smile fade. Quickly regrouping, I rejoined the present conversation, departing from the inner dialogue going on in my head with one last thought. *No doubt, Estelle could never replace her but fill in the gaps? "This" Evie knew Estelle could do.*

She promised herself to help make this happen. Rick would certainly appreciate her efforts as well. Estelle and he had already experienced enough turmoil in their lives together. Evie wasn't about to add any more. "There was no place for such silliness," she decided. It was something she hoped Baron would eventually realize too.

"Saul," Estelle called, launching into a completely different topic. "Rick wants to know how Evie might go about converting to Judaism. Do you have any idea?"

Saul, easily being the most observant Jew in the family, was more apt to know that answer than anyone else. Estelle was very proud of him for this, despite the challenges posed by differing levels of Jewish adherence under one roof. They made their relationship work, regardless.

"It's not an easy process," Saul replied while shaking his head. "But if you have the right Rabbi involved, it's a doable one. I'd suggest we speak to Rabbi Silberman. He can help us."

"Thanks Saul," I said.

"Yes, thanks Saul," Rick added.

"My pleasure, you two. Now, all this talk about conversion... when's the wedding?"

Rick and I looked at each other in unison. "I haven't asked her yet," Rick replied.

"Well, what are you waiting for, mister? Do it before I ask her myself. I've been thinking about getting me a new wife. The one I have right now is growing a bit old," Saul replied with a wink.

"Old?" Estelle cried, picking up a napkin and tossing it across the table. It landed perfectly on Saul's plate as if to emphasize how outlandish his teasing actually was. Estelle snickered, quite familiar with Saul's Vaudeville-type humor and the rise he always tried to get out of her.

Rick laughed at the two of them, then remarked, "That would be smart, now wouldn't it?"

"It would, darling," Estelle chimed in. "Saul's right...plus I'm looking forward to some grandbabies."

"Notice she said grandbabies...with an "S," Saul continued. "You best do it sooner rather than later in my opinion. You know your mother."

"Oh, yes, Saul. That I do." Rick replied, sarcastically. He flashed his mom a loving smile to assure her of his intentions.

Estelle just rolled her eyes.

By this time, I thought that they had forgotten that I was in the room, so carried away had they become in their banter.

I couldn't help but think about how different this evening had been compared to the one Rick and I had experienced a few nights earlier. *Worlds apart,* I thought to myself as I hugged Estelle and Saul good-bye. I was looking forward to seeing both of them again and made sure Rick knew so on the way home.

The following day, Estelle called me to arrange an afternoon of lunch and shopping. It was one of the best days I would ever share with her, leaving me even more excited to embrace her as my mom just as much as Rick's. "When?" was the only question that remained.

Chapter 6

The Proposal

Over the next month, it seemed that Rick's and my life together went into overdrive. So many monumental changes occurred. I moved in with him fully, quit my job, and concentrated on pulling together the marketing program for the new software company Rick wanted to launch. And we began conversion classes.

I was learning to read, write and speak Hebrew while receiving a rapid education in Jewish culture, religion, and traditions. Classes met once a week for three hours at a time and Rick was required to attend them with me. Every Wednesday evening we'd take the long drive to Redbank, New Jersey, eating sandwiches that I had made for supper in the car. We'd gab about the upcoming class, the other classmates, and all that we had learned already. It seemed that Rick was absorbing just as much as I was. It made me feel even closer to him and our future, more real.

Rick continued to work at his father's company during the day. At night, however, he began writing the software program he planned to launch his new venture around. The deal was that I would handle the marketing side of the business, having graduated with that degree, and seemingly—very good at it. Rick would concentrate on the technology side, including designing and implementing the software as well as consulting. We were becoming real partners, professionally, just as we had become personally.

I wanted to help Rick make his dream come true because, I knew, he had already made mine. I loved him more than I could have ever imagined loving a man. I also saw this business as our foundation and road to freedom, allowing Rick to get out from underneath his father both quickly and permanently. Having labeled our conversation "a complete misunderstanding" when speaking with Rick about it, Baron was certain to deny future meddling in the same way. I knew that I couldn't trust him, especially now. His input would be detrimental to Rick's and my happiness.

I wasn't alone in my thinking. A very close friend and former college professor of Rick's, Dr. Shirley McGovern, wholeheartedly agreed. Dr. McGovern was well acquainted with the *Barons* of the world. The youngest female Senior Vice President in a Fortune 500 company when few were to be had, this woman was clearly no dummy.

It was during one of our visits to her home in Glens Falls, New York, that I stole a few private moments away with her and recanted the tale of what I had experienced at Baron's home. As we strolled across the campus in which she taught, we stopped at the foot of a building. She pointed out the name born across the front of it, "The Baron L. Remington School Of Technology."

There wasn't much left to discuss after that. She had encapsulated Baron's entire personality in the pointing of a single finger. He was a man used to getting what he wanted. "Go quietly," he wouldn't, especially when he had an empire hanging in the balance.

"Don't lose heart however, Evie. Rick isn't stupid, and he is just as determined. You are a very special woman, and he knows it," Dr. McGovern said.

It was later that year when I learned of her hand in my engagement to Rick. Pulling him aside before we departed for back home that weekend, she advised Rick with absolute adamance to "close the deal," meaning to...*propose now you dummy!*

"Close before she knows what hit her," were her exact words to Rick as he recalled. The fact was Dr. McGovern understood the extent of Rick's downside as much as his upside and she was convinced that grabbing me while I was still blissfully in love and blind to my future realities was the intelligent thing to do. Sounds cunning, I know. But it wasn't meant to be. Dr. McGovern wanted the best for Rick and me. The shove had come from a good place, merely meant to get the ball rolling.

To this day I marvel at just how brilliant this woman had been, although I dare say, I would have married Rick even with a worse downside. Dr. McGovern would ultimately become someone whose support I sincerely appreciated, especially upon hearing the story of how she aided Rick in his decision to propose, the extent of which was exaggerated by Rick beyond belief. As Rick would tell it, "She gave me no choice. It was either marry you or tell Pop that she would no longer be teaching at his namesake's school. What was I to do?"

"I'm glad she talked such sense into you," I blurted out sarcastically, playing along with his self-indulgent farce.

Rick snickered.

Dr. McGovern and I chatted regularly after that weekend, becoming good friends just as she and Rick had been. I especially called upon her when I felt the need for professional advice. Building a new business was a bit overwhelming as was working from home. No doubt, doing so made balancing the sudden changes and newfound responsibilities in my life a whole lot easier. Multitasking between household chores and canvassing for consulting opportunities for Rick became a breeze, but I missed regular contact with co-workers. So I offset my isolation with daily phone calls to friends.

I knew Rick appreciated all that I was doing as he told me so thousands of times, including through simple, inexpensive gestures that meant the world to me. He'd leave me cards to find after he left for the day, write me poetry, and surprise me with little tokens of his affection.

One such trinket, a ceramic peapod, opened to reveal two green peas inside. I fell in love with that thing, so cute were they as was the meaning behind. When Rick gave it to me he remarked, "Exactly like us, I believe...two peas in a pod." I couldn't have agreed more. I set it on the nightstand next to my side of the bed. Somehow, however, I inadvertently knocked it off during the following week as I went about my usual cleaning. Doing so evoked quite an unexpected stir.

The apartment had become a mess and me, the clean freak, wasn't about to let it get much more out of control. So I began to dust, and that's when I must have hit it. When I finally realized, I anxiously dropped to my knees, hoping to find it under the bed, no doubt accompanying a ton of dust bunnies there too.

I was almost entirely right. I did find the pea pod but not among any dust bunnies but leaning up against a small black suitcase. Immediately, my curiosity got the better of me. I pulled the suitcase out from underneath, popped open the latches and looked inside. I couldn't believe my eyes.

The suitcase was filled with money, stacks of bills of all different sizes—tens, twenties, fifties, hundreds and larger. *What was Rick doing with all of this cash*? I thought to myself. *Hmmm,* I continued. Whatever it was, I knew that I needed to trust him.

Closing the suitcase, I slipped it back under the bed where I had discovered it and never said a word to Rick. The fact of the matter was, I did trust Rick. So, if he felt the need to keep a suitcase full of money under the bed, I was sure he had a very good reason.

"Child...don't tell me Rick was dealing drugs," Debra cried.

"No. Nothing like that," I replied. "But he definitely had a scheme up his sleeve."

"Thank goodness," she said. "I thought you were going to tell me something I didn't want to hear. By the way, any chance I can get some ice for my foot and two Tylenol if you have them? It's beginning to throb."

"Absolutely," I readily replied.

"I'm truly sorry for the inconvenience," Debra continued.

"Think nothing of the sort," I answered, handing her an ice pack, the two Tylenol and a glass of water. "Anything else while I'm up?"

"No thank you, dear," Debra responded. "Keep going. I'm eager to hear more about the suitcase. What happened next?"

Well, a few days went by. Having decided to try to forget about it, I went on with my life in a "business as usual" kind of way. Then midway through Friday afternoon, Rick rang me from the office and asked if I could meet him at Firenze's for dinner. It was one of our favorite restaurants as the food was incredible but the decor was rather fancy so we rarely went. Rick sounded in a really good mood however and told me that we had something exceedingly important to celebrate.

Getting ready, I pulled on a simple black dress. Estelle had picked it out for me during one of our shopping excursions. She had incredible style and was teaching me the finer points of dressing as well. Then I adjusted my makeup and curled my hair. I loved special evenings like this one even though I had no idea what was going on. To me, it was fun, including whenever I saw Rick's eyes light up the moment I entered the room.

Trying to figure out what it was that we had to celebrate while heading to the restaurant, I was concerned that I might have forgotten an important date. But, after reviewing my mental calendar, nothing stood out. *I guess it's something new,* I thought. I was eager to hear the news.

Once inside, I saw Rick arranging a table with the hostess. *God, that man is handsome,* I thought to myself, then stopped. *Jews don't do that,* meaning use the word "God" in regular conversation as I had become accustomed to doing growing up. *You have to try harder.* Vowing that I would, I made my way to Rick and cupped my hands over his eyes. He slid my right hand down upon his lips and kissed it. "Hi beautiful," he said.

"Great, she's here," the hostess remarked. "Right this way."

She brought us to the furthest table in the restaurant. It was dark and extremely intimate. I could hear Andrea Bocelli singing one of my favorite romantic ballads, IL Correggio Di Vivere, in the background. Rick pulled out my chair and I sat down. Then taking a seat across from me, he complimented me on my new dress. "You look stunning," he said.

"Thank your mom," I replied. "She picked it out."

"I should actually be thanking your mom," Rick answered, then continued. "Evie, you are the most beautiful woman in the world, and I can't imagine ever being without you."

My radar bolted up. The hostess was nowhere to be seen and

surveying the room, neither was anyone else for that matter. "Was this it?" I cried inside. "Was he going to propose?"

Suddenly, Rick stood up from his chair, moved over to my side of the table and bent down on one knee. My heart began to race. I stood staring at him, frightened and excited all at the same time. "Evie," he began, his voice shaking. "Will you..."

Before he could even get another word out of his mouth, our waitress showed up without warning. Having waltzed over to the table in a daze, she didn't even notice Rick midway through his proposal and completely missed that he was down on one knee.

Rick looked up at her in complete disbelief. "Could you possibly give us a minute?" he politely asked. Suddenly realizing what she had just done, she quickly apologized and rushed out of the room.

"Now where were we?" Rick continued, feeling confident that another interruption would not be forthcoming. "Evie, my love, will you marry me?"

It took all of two seconds for me to answer. "Yes," I screamed. "Absolutely."

Rick pulled a velvet box from his pocket and, still on one knee, directed me to open it. Inside, sat a four-carat diamond ring. It was spectacular and even more so because—as I learned later—he had designed it himself. I couldn't believe my eyes nor my incredible good fortune. This ring was mine. He was mine. I felt like the luckiest woman in the world.

"Do you like it?" he questioned.

"It's perfect," I cried.

"Let's put it on you," he said.

Handing Rick the box, he removed the ring from inside, gently guided my hand towards his and slipped it on the traditional fourth finger. I marveled at how the diamonds sparkled. Then jumping to my feet, I pulled him up to his and kissed him passionately.

The entire room broke out in applause, signaling the waitress to bring over two glasses of champagne.

"Sorry about before," she stated. She couldn't have been more embarrassed.

"No problem," Rick replied.

The rest of the evening was spent discussing the ruse he and Estelle had pulled off. Committed to designing a one-of-a-kind ring for me, Rick had spent several evenings drafting all types of designs as opposed to the software programs I thought he had been working on.

"I got those done too," he stated, "but Estelle needed some sort of idea of what I actually wanted so that she could bring it to her friend, Mel Lehman, who owns a store downtown, in the diamond district. Once we agreed upon a price, he got to work. I met him in the city today to pick up the ring," he said.

"Having agreed to pay him in cash, I needed to bring that to him as well and confirm that everything was exactly as I had expected it to be. It was. I was so excited to give it to you that I couldn't wait any longer. I am so glad you like it, Evie."

"Like it?" I blurted out. "It is the most incredible engagement ring I've ever seen!

"See," he replied. "And you never even suspected that I had hidden the money to pay for it right under our bed."

I could barely hold my laughter in as I pondered how proudly Rick had just delivered that statement. Having no idea who was actually fooling whom in this charade, I chose to join in on it rather than steal his thunder and reveal the truth of the matter.

"No, I didn't," I said. "You definitely tricked me." It was the only white lie I would ever tell Rick for the rest of our lives together.

The entire evening was a night to remember. Every moment of it took on a whole new meaning, including making love to him when we returned home. This time, I was doing so as his future wife. I desired his touch even more, realizing fully that he would be the only man ever to push his way inside me again. I craved him, uncontrollably, wanting to 'seal the deal' by arousing him into a sexual frenzy. Then opening my legs, I could feel his hard, warm penis explode, making me moan with ecstasy.

Rick continued to lie on top of me for some time after that. Then shifting positions, he wrapped himself around me and pulled me to him. "Good night, my future wife," he whispered, lovingly.

"Good night, my future husband. I love you," I replied.

Everything I had ever wanted was now coming true. I could hardly believe it. The surrealness seemed incomparable. No more "being alone." No more "hoping." This was my reality and nothing could have made me happier.

"I love you too," he said. Then, in Rick's own unique and *incorrigible* way, he reminded me of the very words that he had shared on our way home from Baron's house months prior. "You see, Evie," he explained. "Be careful what you wish for."

I reflected upon those words for a moment, contemplating how true they had become. Then closing my eyes, I joined Rick in perfect slumber.

Chapter 7

The Ultimatum

"They're engaged!" Estelle screamed, waving the phone in the air. "Saul, did you hear me?"

"The entire neighborhood heard you, Estelle," Saul replied as he briskly entered the room. "So, the boy, finally, wisened up. Good for him...and you, my darling. Mazel Tov." He kissed Estelle on the cheek as he chuckled at his wife's ecstatic state. Eyeing a pot of freshly brewed coffee, Saul picked up a mug from the drying rack and filled it. Then turning back towards Estelle, he asked, "Has the happy couple set a date?"

"They are thinking this spring," Estelle replied, beaming.

"This spring?" Saul repeated. "That's right around the corner. Will she be converted by then?"

"Rick assures me she will."

"Let's check with the Rabbi just to make sure that he's on the same page." Then pulling his cell phone out of his pocket, Saul began dialing Rabbi Silberman.

"They're on their way to tell Baron now," said Estelle.

Saul answered from the side of his mouth, "That should be some conversation."

Estelle nodded in agreement. "Yes, it should."

"Hello Rabbi. It's Saul Klein. Have you heard the good news?" Saul shuffled back to his chair in the living room, plopped down, and began taking care of business.

We spent the ride to the cafe where we were to meet Baron and his new girlfriend discussing all sorts of wedding plans. We knew that Rabbi Silberman would preside and that we were going to include some old-fashioned Jewish traditions in the ceremony. These involved my circling the groom three times, the exchange of plain wedding bands, and the stomping of the glass at the end of it by Rick. But past that, the rest needed to be worked out.

We both knew that we didn't want to have a big wedding, preferring an intimate affair to the circus that seems to have become quite common these days. We wanted our wedding to remain about "us" and shared with those who cared most about our happiness together.

"We will find the right place, Evie," Rick said.

"Rick, as long as I am with you, we could get married in our apartment," I replied, knowing full well that that wouldn't happen but feeling perfectly content if it did. "Evie Remington," I kept repeating over and over to myself. "I just love that name."

"Here we are," Rick interrupted. "Le Petite Pistache." Hopping from the car and moving around to my side, Rick opened my door and waited for me to join him outside. A wave of nervousness washed over me as I grabbed my bag and rose to my feet. This was only the second time I would see Baron and, as the first time hadn't gone so well, I was praying that the second time would go much better.

"Come on Sweetie. Time to tell Pop."

Rick and I walked into the restaurant and recognized Baron seated at a table by one of the windows. A lovely looking woman was sitting next to him. She had bright orange hair and blue eyes—very pretty and surprisingly older than either Rick or I had expected.

Recognizing us, Baron waved. *Here we go*, I thought, clutching Rick's hand tightly.

"Ah, my boy," Baron said, rising and hugging Rick. "Evie, dear, how are you?" Baron asked, a pleasant smile affixed to his face. I walked over and gave him the obligatory hug and then remained standing to be introduced to the newest lady in his life. "Rick, Evie, this is Shannon."

"Very nice to meet you both," said Shannon in a thick Irish brogue.

"Likewise," Rick replied.

Rick pulled out my chair and I sat down. He followed, quickly, behind. "So where did you two meet?" Rick continued.

"We met when I was on my way back from my last trip to Ireland. Since then, we've kept in touch and now she's here. Isn't that great?" Baron looked enormously pleased.

"Yes, Pop," Rick replied. "Absolutely great."

"How long will you be staying?" I broke in, directing my question to Shannon.

"Just a few days," Shannon responded. "Your dad is coming back with me next week."

"Yup," Baron said. "I'm taking a vacation."

"You? A vacation? Wow, that's news," Rick piped up. "I can't remember the last time you did that, Pop. Good for you," he continued.

"Yes, it's been a while. If I remember straight, my last vacation was when you and Cindy joined me for a few days on our yacht in the Caribbean. It was a fun time. Whatever happened to that girl, by the way? I always liked her. Nice Jewish roots and smart as a whip. Her dad was in toilet paper from what I recall. Made a mint."

"I don't know nor do I care," replied Rick expeditiously, hoping to squelch the tension rising inside me as he felt my grip tighten upon his forearm. "And anyway, Pop, we have much better things to discuss. We have some news of our own that Evie and I want to tell you. Really good news."

"Well, what is it, my boy? I can't wait to hear." Baron leaned forward in his seat.

His full attention now captured, Rick announced, "Evie and I are engaged. We are getting married."

By this time, my heart was in my throat. My eyes must have looked like saucers to Baron as he sat across the table, allowing the news to sink in.

"Congratulations," Shannon cried, not realizing the volatility of the situation she unknowingly was swept up into by her mere presence.

Baron smiled accordingly, then remarked, "I hope you two lovebirds will be very happy together."

Waving the waiter to his side, Baron ordered a bottle of their best champagne. Within minutes the goblets were filled, and Baron was toasting to the future of me and Rick. It seemed as if the worst was over. I was wrong, however. It had only just begun. What happened next, nobody could have predicted.

"Evie, my dear, you will have to give me the name and number of your attorney," Baron stated.

"My attorney?" I replied, having absolutely no idea what Baron was talking about nor the reason he was asking.

"Yes, dear," he continued. "Someone is going to need to review the prenup."

I felt like I had just been shot. I turned to Rick, who seemed to have the same look on his face as me. "Rick," I said. "What prenup?"

"I have no idea," Rick replied. "Pop, what are you talking about? David, Elliot and their wives don't have prenuptial agreements."

"No, they don't, my boy...but you will," he said sternly. "Rick, you have a ton to lose and the rest of the family has even more with you getting married. Remember our agreement."

"Remember that I told you that I didn't want to take over the companies. I'm building my own company now with Evie's help."

"Even more reason to have one," Baron growled.

Shannon fell completely silent. A smart woman, she figured out what was going on quickly.

Anger flowed through every artery and vein in me. I couldn't believe my ears. And I couldn't just sit there while Baron pushed his weight around. A precedent needed to be set and now was the time to do it.

Bracing myself for the fallout, I said, "Baron, I am not signing any prenuptial agreement unless Rick wants me to. You can take that to the bank."

Baron cried out, "What? Do you think I owe you a living?" His venomous expression was unlike any I'd ever seen before.

Carefully, I continued, "No, Baron. You don't...but then again, I'm not marrying you." In urgency, I jumped to my feet.

Then turning towards Shannon, I said calmly, "and I'd suggest you don't either." With that, I marched out of the restaurant and headed towards the car.

"Great job, Pop. Thanks." Rick followed me out the door. When he found me, my face was drenched with tears.

I screamed out, "Did you know about this?"

"No, Evie. I swear. I had no idea."

"Is that what you want? Do you want me to sign a prenuptial agreement?"

"Evie, if I wanted you to sign a prenup, I wouldn't have asked you to marry me," Rick replied, embracing me in his arms as he did. "I trust you."

I hugged him tightly back. Feeling a bit more settled, I apologized for questioning him. Rick understood and assured me that his father would rethink the entire matter, and all would be forgotten by tomorrow.

"Unfortunately, that wasn't exactly what happened either," I said to Debra.

"What happened?" Debra replied, holding her breath in anticipation.

"Rick returned home early from work the subsequent Monday. Baron had not only fired him but disinherited him. Baron also barred Rick from attending all family events held at the family home."

"That bastard," Debra cried.

"Yes, he was," I agreed. "Rick was beyond angry as well as feeling quite a bit of pain."

The stress of being ostracized like this caused his Crohn's disease to flare up. He spent the rest of the day resting in bed. It was the first time I had ever seen Rick struggle with his disease. I felt terrible for him and did everything that I could to comfort him. Then when he finally fell asleep, I moved my computer over to the bed, sat next to him, and began marketing the hell out of the services Rick's new company would offer.

The next day, he got his first big call. I answered it while staring at two brilliantly colored cardinals sitting on the railing outside our living room window. It was at that moment that I knew everything would be alright. That WE were going to be alright.

Baron's second miscalculation would, ultimately, result in an impenetrable bond between Rick and me few couples ever knew and certainly not Baron. "He would realize it over time," I said to myself as I carried my phone to the bedroom and handed it to Rick.

It was a brand new day in the "House of Remington," I thought, drawing a dollar sign into the air and smiling.

Rick sat up, grinned, then retrieved the phone.

That call marked the actual beginning of Rick's new venture, with many clients to come. Baron could do nothing about it. We could finally move ahead, untethered, making our life everything that we wanted it to be and more. Frankly, we had it all and we had just started. In time, much, much more would come.

Chapter 8

The Wedding

"Are you ready?" Rabbi Silberman asked.

"I am," I replied, confidently. Rick, Saul and Estelle were watching me—three witnesses that could attest to my legitimate entrance into the Jewish faith. My conversion classes completed, it was now time to make it official. Teaneck, New Jersey, would be the location of my religious rebirth. As my mother had grown up there, the coincidence seemed nothing of the sort and rather apropos.

"Estelle, please follow Evie into the next room to observe her descent into the Mikvah."

It was a surprise out of left field shared with me just that morning. The usual witness that would watch me strip down naked and enter the pool of water fell sick that day. Short of a replacement, Estelle had volunteered to stand in. My future mother-in-law would now see "the goods." *There'd be no turning back after that*, I thought.

It was a bonding moment that cemented my conversion, my love for her son, and my full appreciation of Estelle.

"Don't worry, dear," she said. "I will shut my eyes."

I blushed anyway. Twenty minutes later, I emerged from the dressing room fully clothed and fully Jewish. Rick kissed me. Saul hugged me crying out, "Mazel Tov." And Estelle beamed from ear to ear. The deed was done and the wedding, just around the corner. I couldn't wait. We celebrated over a nice lunch, filled with discussion about Rick's and my wedding plans.

Estelle had helped me arrange almost everything. The French Chateau, the simple fare, the flowers, the music, the cake, the dress. The only thing completely left to my own devices was the wedding invitation, which I designed myself, using characters that I had created as a child called "The Flumps." They were silly but they were also quite personal to me, having created them in the aftermath of losing my mom. Somehow they seemed to help me through that time, bringing moments of solace and joy where there was little for many years following her passing.

Rick loved the idea of each of us contributing something unique to the wedding celebration. Mine would be the invitation and in that, I'd feel as if my mom had had a hand in our wedding plans too. Rick continued to remind me that she had, having contributed the bride, the central element to the entire event. But I wanted something more, something beyond the obvious. What could be better than the wedding invitations? I couldn't think of anything.

Rick's contribution would be the way we would cut the cake—using an enormous sword he'd picked up at an antique shop years earlier. Needless to say, it didn't impress the in-house chef, who doubled as the in-house baker too; nor please him in the least. It downright frightened him, in fact. Visions of his masterpiece being mangled by a sword wasn't anything he welcomed when it came to his art. The guests loved it anyway, as Rick had suspected they would.

The Wedding

Having sent the wedding invitations out a month prior, we had already received most of our responses back. I was waiting for just a few to finalize the seating chart. One of those was Baron's. "His" I sent within the first batch that went to the post. Along with the invitation, I enclosed a handwritten note, assuring him that we wanted him there and that Rick missed him greatly. The rest of the family seemed undisturbed by the cold shoulder Baron had been giving to Rick and me. We still saw everyone regularly just not in his company. That said, Rick was pained by the separation, and I wanted Baron to realize this and come to his senses and the wedding.

When Baron's response finally arrived, I couldn't believe my eyes or nose for that matter. I opened the envelope to find the response card bearing a big fat "No" on it. What's worse, it had been slathered with dog shit.

"What!" Debra screamed. "He returned the invitation with dog poop on it?"

"Not the invitation," I replied. "The response card and yes, all over almost every inch of it. It broke my heart to show Rick."

"That man is nuts!" Debra shrieked. "You're lucky that he didn't come to the wedding."

"Even so," I said. "Rick was upset. It didn't dampen our wedding day any, but it did cause Rick to have another Crohn's attack, one more severe than the last."

"That poor boy. I thought I'd seen it all, but this man takes the cake."

"Yes, he did, and he missed it too as well as a wonderful wedding to boot. It couldn't have been more perfect and at the end of it, I was Rick's wife."

"Lucky man," Debra said, then continued, "Where'd you go

for your honeymoon?"

"Disneyworld," I cried "and then we took a two-week cruise in the Caribbean. The first thing Estelle asked us when we returned was not "if we had had a good time" but if we were pregnant yet."

"Boy, that lady sure does love those babies," Debra chuckled.

"Yes, she does," I smiled. "Still to this day. She speaks to all of them regularly, especially the girls. She's exceptionally good at broaching touchy topics when I can't seem to and sharing stories about their dad."

"Grandmas can be best friends with grandkids. Mothers...not so much. They need to be more," Debra explained, obviously understanding this struggle quite well. Most women did in some way or another.

"I get that but sometimes I wish things could be different. We get the saucy, and they get the gravy, so to speak." I laughed at my own cleverness.

Debra did too. "Ain't that the truth," she replied. "Girls."

"Girls," I copied, nodding my head in the process. "Perfect, difficult, and you can't live without them is how Rick used to describe us."

"That statement alone explains why the man you married was such a gem," Debra retorted. "Men aren't always so accepting or astute, especially when they are young. Some are but many aren't."

"Most men had little on Rick. In fact, none did. That's the reason why I was so proud to marry him and be his wife for all those years," I answered. "Which doesn't mean roses bloomed every minute throughout our marriage or even every minute of the entire first year, mind you. It just means that I wouldn't have traded him in for another."

"So you were happy like you thought you would be?" Debra answered.

"Yes, I was," I replied.

"So then tell me about it. What happened? What went wrong in paradise?"

I leaned back, placed my hands over my eyes then sighed. I needed that pause to continue. Then rubbing my face, I moved my hands to the table once again and began. The hardest part of my journey as well as "Rick's and my story" was about to be told.

Patient and bewildered, Debra could feel the mood in the room shift, compelling her to do the same. Readjusting herself in her seat as if to brace herself for what was about to come, she settled in for a second time and waited for me to continue. Not wanting to re-ask the question, she just sat, staring me down until I could no longer take it.

I couldn't bridle my words from that point on. I didn't. Debra wanted to know what had happened to my beautiful life with Rick, and I wasn't about to keep it from her. I was proud of it, saddened by it, and missing it still. Sharing our tale made me feel better, helped me to heal. The healing never ended. I'd come to accept this.

Debra said to me that *she wasn't so sure about that.* She listened anyway, making more sense of my life with every syllable. She had not expected any of what I would tell her but, then again, neither did I when it happened. It just happened. And then I just hung on for dear life. "Not doing so" was never an option.

Chapter 9

The Anniversary

I planned to wake up early. Having already retrieved the top tier of our wedding cake from the freezer the night before, I wanted to surprise Rick with breakfast in bed complete with orange juice, blueberry coffee, the cake and two forks. I also wanted to give him a special gift that I had found to celebrate our full year together. It was a handsome mezuzah handcrafted by one of his favorite artists. It looked very "art deco" in design, very appropriate to Rick's taste.

When I found it, I knew it was perfect for him. At some point, we would have a house and what better way to bless it than to adorn the front entry with a gift that honored our beginning, our love, and our newly shared faith.

Rick had a plan of his own however and it ended up being his plan that set the stage for the rest of the day. Waking me with that same tray filled with orange juice, mugs of coffee, cake and a rose to boot, he kissed me gently on the forehead while whispering, "Snuggs, it's time to get up."

It was five-thirty in the morning on a Saturday, barely daybreak. It was unusual for Rick to be up so early on the weekend.

I guess he's excited to share the day, I thought. I turned myself over onto my back, pulled myself up into a sitting position, and leaned against my pillow and the headboard.

He kissed me again, this time on my lips and said, "Happy Anniversary, my wonderful wife." His face was beaming. He seemed completely elated. It was the most adorable display of absolute bliss that I could have ever hoped for. He hopped back into bed, picked up a big bite of cake with a fork and shoved it into my mouth. I almost choked from the size of it. I began gagging as it managed to find its way down the wrong pipe. Rick grabbed a glass of juice and handed it to me. "Sorry Snuggs."

"Don't worry about it," I forced. I picked up a fork of my own and filled it with an even larger piece of cake and shoved it into his mouth. "I know you are trying to kill me," I teasingly said. "It's only been one year."

"The best year of my life," he replied. He swallowed his piece effortlessly. I grinned. Stretching my arm over my head as to shake off the stiffness it was feeling, I continued the motion and slyly reached under the bed. When my arm returned, his gift was in my hand.

"Sorry, I'm just too excited to wait until tonight at dinner." I had arranged to return to the scene of the crime, Firenze's, to celebrate our first year as an old, married couple. I even asked for the same table and the same waitress to wait on us, the one who had interrupted Rick mid-proposal.

"I didn't realize you had made those plans," Rick replied, taking the gift from my hand and eagerly tearing the paper from it. As he did, he continued nonchalantly, "You will have to cancel them."

He pulled the mezuzah from the box and admired every inch of it. "I love it, Evie. Thank you. I'm gonna save it for our first house." Undoubtedly, we thought alike. To that end, however, I had no idea what he was thinking when suggesting that I needed to cancel our dinner reservation.

I responded in a bit of a confused manner, "I am really glad you love it Rick but what do you mean that I need to cancel tonight? I don't understand."

"I know you don't," Rick snickered. "But you will in about eight hours from now. The car arrives in thirty minutes," he continued. "Pack a light bag as we're not checking luggage. You need a few bathing suits, shorts, tops and one or two dresses. You can call Firenze's and cancel before we board the plane."

"The plane," I remarked. "Is that why you got me up so early?" I asked, leaping from the bed and rushing to the spare bedroom to grab my suitcase from the closet. A surge of excitement overtook me. I returned, throwing my suitcase at the bottom of Rick's feet. "Oh God; oh God; oh God," I kept repeating. This time, I didn't berate myself for breaking Jewish law. I let my words fly, not having an extra moment to spare to admonish myself.

Rick was chuckling as he observed my every move. "Evie, honey, the car isn't going to leave without us."

"Yes, but the plane will," I replied. "Any chance you are going to tell me where we are going?" I continued, already recognizing that forcing our destination out of him upfront was a long shot.

"Not on your life," he replied, eating the rest of the cake as he watched me run around the apartment like a madwoman.

Arriving back from the bathroom with my makeup case and hairbrush, I screeched at him as I tossed them both inside my handbag. "Why aren't you packing?" He pointed to the side of the dresser below the television. His suitcase stood "ready and waiting."

"I did it two days ago. You never even noticed it was sitting there the entire time."

I shook my head, realizing how oblivious I had been. Unlike "resilience," being aware of my surroundings wasn't another strong suit. *Need to work on that*, I thought.

Before I knew it, the car had arrived, and we were inside. Settling excitedly into our seats for the two hour trip to the airport, Rick handed me a card to open. On the front of it, two cardinals shared a branch and a nuzzle. *More cardinals*, I thought. *There is definitely something to this.* Inside was a lovely saying about love, trust, and forever. But it was Rick's handwritten scribble that sent me to tears. He wrote:

"Evie, You are my world. I fell in love with you the day we met, and I will be in love with you until my dying breath. You may be sick of me after seventy or so years but I will still be head over heels in love with you for sure. And now, since you've given me my world, I want to expand yours. Buckle up. We are going to Jamaica!"

"Jamaica," I squealed. "We are going to Jamaica?" I had never stayed on an island before. Now I was headed to Jamaica with the most wonderful husband on the planet. I couldn't believe my life. Since the moment I'd met Rick, it seemed too good to be true. And the bubble I was living in wasn't bursting; in fact, it just kept getting better. "I will never get sick of you," I whispered in his ear as I wrapped my arms around him and gave him a big hug."

"I hope not," he said. "Also, don't forget to call Firenze's."

Back to business, I picked up my phone and dialed.

By four-thirty that afternoon, we were checked into our bungalow on the beach. Rick had arranged a full week's vacation at the Half Moon Bay Club. It was the newest and nicest resort in Montego Bay, complete with tennis courts, our own pool, and four incredible restaurants, every one of them no less than five stars. It was also close to the local market where Rick would continue to give me lessons regarding "how to negotiate."

He was a master, having spent many years watching Baron wheel and deal. Rick had said once that the toughest people to negotiate with were the Chinese as they had all types of tactics to understand before you walked into the room; otherwise, you'd lose your shirt. They also had their own way of measuring "worthiness." Baron taught Rick every one of them and now he was teaching me.

Our digs for the next seven days were gorgeous. A beautiful rattan bed stood in a large open area. Near it, a bureau, a television, and a desk. In a second room, there was a pretty table in which to eat, with a vase of flowers sitting in the center. Everything we need-ed to nestle in comfortably for the week was placed conveniently on the cabinet near the table. We needn't leave the bungalow if we didn't want to. The bathroom was enormous too. A big tub with a basket full of goodies called to the both of us as we surveyed our surroundings.

"What do you think, Snuggs?" I heard Rick shout from the bathroom. By now I was changing out of my travel clothes and into something less sweaty. I'd then unpack the two of us.

"I think I like being Mrs. Remington," I shouted in return. I walked over to the doors off the bedroom and swung both open fully. As the waves came rushing into the shore and flattened them-selves across the sand, I couldn't help but think about "how simple happiness could be with the right person in your life."

I surveyed every inch of the beach in front of me. It was stun-ning. Taking a seat in one of the patio chairs, I studied the horizon. Rick joined me, baring two glasses of cold champagne and a platter of fruits and sweets.

"Compliments of the resort," he noted. Handing me a glass, Rick raised his and stated, "To us, Evie. I promise you, it will just keep getting better."

We sealed his toast with a kiss then spent the rest of the evening chowing down on fresh seafood followed by a very romantic bubble bath and a bedtime escapade that forced the bed to completely reposition itself in the room by the next morning. We woke to have to push it back against the wall from where it had escaped.

We spent the next few days luxuriating in the sun, consuming plates of fiery jerk chicken, shopping, dressing for elegant dinners, swimming, and touring the island. Each evening, we made love and every morning, we did too. The island heat had nothing on the two of us nor the notion that life could get more wonderful as Rick had stated in his toast. Question him, I wouldn't however, especially when "right" seemed so darn superb.

Joining Rick on the patio after just completing a call with one of his clients, I asked, "Everything good at home?" meaning with the business.

Rick answered. "Everything is perfect. In fact, when we return, our biggest account wants to increase our hours. It may mean hiring another consultant. We will see. In the meantime, my darling…"

Before I knew it, Rick rose from his chair and swooped me up into his arms. Carrying me inside and over to the bed, his passionate plans immediately switched to shrieks of pain. He dropped me onto the bed with a thud.

"What happened to my prince?" I joked, not thinking that what was occurring was more than a pebble that had mistakenly caught itself under Rick's heel.

Rick fell onto the bed next to me, gripping his stomach. "My

Crohn's is acting up. It's been doing it all morning. I didn't want to tell you. The pain is the worst it's been. I need my meds."

Scrambling to the bathroom, I grabbed the many bottles he had brought with him. By the time I returned, Rick had crawled underneath the blankets. I opened the bottles and handed him the tiny capsules. He swallowed them down without any water.

"Give me another two of the orange ones," he cried. I did as he asked, knowing exactly which pills he meant. Having been through this with him more than once already, I understood his need to reduce the inflammation quickly to relieve his cramping. Worried and wanting to help him as much as I could, I returned to the bathroom where I grabbed a washcloth, soaked it in the sink, and brought it back to the bed. I laid it on his head, then spent the next hour scratching his back lightly until he fell asleep.

The episode ended up being so severe that we couldn't return home on the day originally planned. Rick couldn't travel. Thankfully, the resort could accommodate us for another week, much of which I spent on my own. I watched over him as he slept. Brought him bottles of water and medicine when he needed them; then, later food when he could eat.

Sitting on the beach in the sun just steps from our bungalow, I occupied myself by drawing my Flumps and reading. And when Rick was feeling better but not good enough to go out yet, I visited the marketplace alone and practiced negotiating. I made many new friends on those days, returning to Rick with more loot and a bunch of great stories to share.

On the final Friday of our extended vacation, Rick joined me at the market to meet the ladies that I had told him about. One, a heavyset woman with eleven kids, said to him in a very 'matter of fact' tone, "You take good care of this woman, you hear me? Don't you leave her after you get her pregnant. You be a good husband and father. Too many men leave. It's not right. Hard on the kids too. Understand?"

Rick nodded, acknowledging the seriousness of what this woman was saying. Then handing her ten dollars, while taking a straw hat from her hand, he replied. "Don't you worry. I will never leave her."

She could see by his face that he meant it, then handed him a pipe to keep as well. "Smoke this the day your first baby comes. It will drive the bad spirits away."

Rick and I both thanked her. Then turning to walk back to the hotel, Rick whispered to me, "Someone should have given one of these to Pop's mom before he was born."

I shook my head and unexpectedly snorted at his humor. *Baron was still very much on Rick's mind and he always would be,* I thought to myself. I had suspected that this had been part of the reason for Rick's sudden Crohn's attack but now I knew for sure. Somehow this fissure needed to be repaired before it impacted Rick's health any further but what to do? I didn't have any answers.

What I did have was plenty of time to think about it during our return flight home as well as the pertinent question, "What would make Baron "open the door" without requiring Rick to kick me through it and out the other side?"

It was a quandary, indeed. One whose solution would eventually show itself with no help from me. This wasn't the case for Rick however, anything but.

Rick would have a profound hand in Baron's return, a *profound* hand indeed...to my dismay.

Chapter 10

The Appointment

Two days after our return from Jamaica, we met with Dr. Crohn. He was able to slip us into his schedule at the last minute. For a doctor as world-renowned as Dr. Crohn, this rarely happened. Dr. Crohn however was extremely concerned with what Rick had already told him about his most recent attack. He wanted to examine him thoroughly and not postpone doing so any longer than truly necessary.

As Rick explained the searing pain further and pointed to the location it had occurred, Dr. Crohn examined the area then presented Rick with his options.

"Look, Rick," he said. "I know we've avoided surgery up to this point, but I really think we can't avoid it anymore. I think we need to remove the area that is acting up now before your flare-ups become worse."

Rick's response to Dr. Crohn's recommendation was a swift and adamant, "No."

He had explained his thinking to me earlier, given the topic of surgery arose. He noted that once "they began cutting, they'd need to continue to do so." He wanted no part of that until all other options were exhausted. He remained firm in his decision.

I didn't know enough about the disease to try to convince him otherwise. That said, the fact that he refused to take Dr. Crohn's advice made me nervous. I felt Rick's decision might be a mistake, but there was no amount of discussion that would change his mind.

Dr. Crohn finally gave up. He offered him another alternative, combining a switch in medication and a further altered diet. It seemed to work well. Rick began to rapidly feel like his old self again. He kept his twice-yearly appointments with Dr. Crohn and underwent imaging whenever necessary.

From that moment on, life returned to normal. Neither of us looked back but for the occasional thought that cropped up inside me, *I guess he knew what he was doing*, meaning Rick in the handling of his disease. It brought me tremendous comfort knowing this and I told him so.

"Yes, I do," he laughed. "You know what I also know, Evie?" he continued. "I know it is time to give Estelle what she has been dreaming of since the day you and I met. I think it is time we try and have a baby."

"Are you serious?" I replied, startled by the suddenness of his suggestion.

"I am," he answered. "I want to be a young dad. I want to take him to the park, play baseball with him, teach him how to sail... you know all those things we've talked about for our future."

"You seem convinced our first child will be a boy," I responded. "What if he's a HER?"

"We will let *her* come too," he teased.

I shook my head, noting the incorrigible nature of this man

hadn't changed one bit in the aftermath of our wedding. Then excitedly, I agreed. "Let the baby-making begin," I shouted as if to announce it to the kingdom.

"And did it?" Debra responded.

"It did," I answered.

"Oh goodie," she replied. "Estelle must have been thrilled."

"She was but we didn't tell her until after we were pregnant. We didn't want that pressure. She needn't wait too long though. We were pregnant within a few months."

"Wow, quick," Debra remarked. "Sometimes it happens that way."

"It did this time as did the terrible morning sickness. The first trimester was sheer hell. All I could eat were bags and bags of grapefruit. It made me feel better. No logic in that, except for the added Vitamin C. The sour taste in my mouth seemed to keep me from vomiting too. Rick ended up keeping sacks of them under the bed. Thankfully, that ended though. My second trimester was much easier," I said.

"It usually is. So many women go through it, and they continue to have babies. It's a wonder...until they put that child in your arms, that is. Then you get it," Debra smiled, reflecting upon her own brood at home.

"Isn't that so," I replied. "They are remarkable. They also change your life rather quickly. They did ours, and Rick figured that out sooner than me."

"How so?" Debra asked.

"Give me a second for a pee break, and I'll tell ya," I replied. "Dashing to the bathroom, I did my business then returned swiftly and continued.

"You definitely broke a record," Debra commented at my

speedy return.

"I only had to pee," I chuckled. "I never understood women who took so long in the bathroom. Never made sense to me. What could they possibly be doing in there?"

"I agree. Another wonder," Debra commented. "Makeup, no doubt."

I shook my head, "Probably. Now, where was I?"

"You were telling me how Rick is smarter than you." Debra mocked, harmlessly.

Raising one eyebrow as to indicate the phrase "Not exactly," I resumed where I'd left off. With so much more to cover, I needed to get a move on. Time was ticking and I could feel my anxiety heighten as I continued to recant the details of my past.

Had it not been for Debra's insistence, I may have left the rest for another day. Taking a break to gather my emotions, might have been kinder...to me, anyway. But I knew the temporary pause wouldn't do for Debra. So I chose to buckle down and keep going.

It wasn't the first time I'd put myself behind another. In fact, the practice had become quite commonplace throughout much of my life with Rick. It was the particular period I was about to describe that punctuated that reality and every day thereafter. I'd learn what "selflessness" really meant, including how the *manner* in which a person chooses to "love" becomes just as much a reflection of her own character as the choice of *whom* to "love," itself.

I learned this because unforeseen circumstances demanded it of me, leaving me no other choice than to indulge them for a while. To be honest, I actually had more choices than I'm letting on, but none of them were palatable in my mind nor would any of them have left me capable of moving forward without being riddled with guilt or regret, I knew. I would have become confined to a prison of my own making. Not wishing this upon myself, I willingly chose to take a "backseat" for as long as I needed to...first to Rick and then ultimately our children. It was the right choice, one I'd make exactly the same way again if I had to.

Chapter 11
The Move

By my fifth month of pregnancy, Rick blurted out, "Honey, I think it's time we got a permanent office."

We were having Shabbat dinner after an extremely busy week. Rick had been managing all fifteen of our company's software developers, programmers and consultants remotely the best that he could, but the company was growing fast. Putting off finding a more suitable location seemed inevitable now, and we both knew it. It was a good problem to have.

"I agree," I remarked. "I can help you look."

"Actually," Rick replied. "Vincent told me that he has an office for rent right around the corner from us. He invited me to look at it tomorrow."

Vincent was our landlord, a lovely gentleman who spoke with a thick Italian accent. Rick could barely understand him when they chatted, but for some reason, I never had a problem.

"Are you sure you understood him correctly?" I grinned, teasingly.

"Yes," Rick replied, overlooking my jab while cutting himself another slice of challah. "My gosh, honey. This challah is great. Where did you get it? A different place than usual?"

"I made it," I replied.

"You made this?" he commented, completely shocked. Knowing the lengthy process that goes into making a loaf of challah, it hadn't occurred to him. Juggling work, life, and pregnancy already took up so much of my time and energy, he knew. *Yet somehow, I squeezed in making challah too.* He was proud but also unwilling to let me off the hook for my prior comment. "That's why I keep you around," he teased.

I accepted his clever response in good spirits...pleased by how improved my culinary skills had become since the day Rachel inadvertently challenged me. By now, she and I shared a very sisterly relationship. In fact, it was Rachel who had given me the recipe for the challah that Rick was devouring.

"Touché," I replied. "Have fun sleeping alone tonight."

"Oh, no you don't." Rick tossed a piece of challah at me that he had ripped from his own. "Make sure that baby is eating...and you," he said with a proud grin. I had already begun showing, and both of us were elated to watch my stomach growing larger every month.

"No worries on that front," I said. My morning sickness now a memory, I was eating well, so well in fact that the doctor asked me to slow down a bit. I found it tough especially with Rick's continual prodding to eat, not to mention Estelle's. I tried hard anyway.

We spent the rest of the evening relaxing together in front of the television. It wasn't long before I was soothed to sleep by the drone of Rick's snoring, a trait that initially caused me many sleepless nights. I'd get used to it over time, however. In some ways, it even comforted me, knowing that "with it, came him."

Soon I'd have a second one of him, I thought to myself as I closed my eyes fully. "How amazing?"

Indeed, it was...remarkably amazing and a bit scary. "We'd handle it together," I always reminded myself when these momentary uncertainties came up. "Like we always did," my parting thought for the day.

We moved into our new office two weeks later. The prior tenant had left most of the furniture so very little furnishing needed to be done, thankfully. So many other things did.

We divided the office in half—the "software and technology" side and the "administrative and marketing" side. Suffice it to say, it wasn't long before both sides were filled, and we began thinking about moving into an even larger space.

The software that Rick had built was in high demand on Wall Street and word traveled fast. It caused Rick's business to grow even faster. Our gamble had paid off and, in some ways, we even felt fortunate for the circumstances that caused Rick to leave his father's business to begin with.

We didn't need Baron to survive and that reality was both empowering and freeing all at the same time. Rick and I had become a strong team. And that "team mentality" showed itself in a variety of different ways, including those following the birth of our first child, a son.

Rick's suspicions had been right all along just as mine had been regarding how wonderful a father he would be. He absolutely loved being a daddy. It was written all over him. Nothing could have been sweeter for me to see. Among the many fatherly attributes that emerged was an undeniably protective nature. I remember one instance in particular that spoke to this. Rick had arranged for us to take a long weekend at The Harborview Hotel in Martha's Vineyard. He chartered a plane for the trip to make it easy on me and the baby.

It was a beautiful place, right on the water with a scenic lighthouse across in the distance. As Rick was checking us in, he learned that the island was anticipating a Nor'easter to hit the following day. Before we were even fully checked-in, Rick "checked us out," literally 'on the spot', not wanting to risk the safety of his new family. We flew home wearing three touristy sweatshirts he had picked up in the hotel store, a bit disappointed but accepting, nonetheless. It ended up being a really bad storm after all, making me grateful for Rick's foresight. It's a story that captures just how easily Rick and I parented together...so easily, in fact, that before long we were eager to have another...and then another...and then another. Once we found our groove, we made the most of it.

Over the next seven years, I gave birth to three more wonderful children—all girls. We moved to a home just up the hill from Estelle and Saul, bought two dogs, and made sure that everything a couple needed to be considered "responsible parents" was in order. This included all of the necessary insurance policies and wills required. Nothing would be left to chance when it came to the welfare of our family and especially our kids.

I must say that I found it quite interesting to contemplate the concept of mortality, his and mine. We seemed to share very different views on the matter. This included the topic of "life support." It's a terrifying reality to think about.

There was no doubt that I wanted to be put out of my misery quickly, for a number of reasons, including not wishing to burden the children in any way. Rick was adamant that he wanted to be kept alive regardless of how long it took to find a cure for his life-threatening malady. I vowed, emphatically, that I would respect his wishes and he did the same. We never discussed the matter again, seeing no need. We had it all—a fairytale lifestyle, healthy children, and a love that remained steadfast. What more could we ask for?

It's an answer we'd soon find out, "the actual question" being one no loving couple or family ever wanted any part of. As "Murphy lived" yet again, this time I could have choked him dead.

Instead, I was forced to choke down catastrophic news that Rick and I were ill-prepared to consume regardless of all *planning* or our ability to handle endless hours of fear and sorrow, both of which became quite familiar, unfortunately. They'd ultimately lose their unnerving grip upon me as a result, making this the first time I'd ever truly meet the woman I was meant to become. In a million years, I couldn't have predicted *her*.

Chapter 12

The Surprise

We were eating dinner. Michael, our oldest, sat munching loudly while excitedly recalling every last detail of his field trip that day between bites. He was in first grade and loved school. A good student and friendly child, Michael could barely get his story out quickly enough or so it seemed.

At the same time, Victoria and Joyce sat content, absorbed by their big brother's every word while scooping up spoonfuls of mac-n-cheese—their favorite. Our youngest child, Grace, was sleeping soundly in her nursery. Only a few weeks old, she was an extremely easy baby from the start—a blessing amid all the usual chaos a large family can bring.

"Do you need anything?" I called to Rick from across the room. He was lying upright on the couch, struggling with the position he currently found himself in as well as the bowl of applesauce that sat on a tray beside him. It was his first meal with the family since his recent surgery. The stress of everyday life—even as wonderful as ours—had taken a toll, causing regular flare-ups of his Crohn's disease now. With Dr. Crohn's further pressing and eventual threats, Rick finally decided to abide by his recommendations. Surgery had become his only option.

Thankfully, the news came during a time when the business was practically running itself. I hadn't worked for the company in years now, preferring to stay home and be with the children. I didn't like the idea of schlepping into the office each day while leaving them with a nanny and neither did Rick. Luckily, we found a great woman to take over my position named Elizabeth Manno. She'd eventually become just as much a member of our family as a fixture at the company.

"No, honey," Rick replied. "I'm not sure that I'm up for eating even this right now."

Joyce hopped down from her chair and bounced over to her father, wrapping her arms around his neck and giving him a great big hug. "I love you, Daddy," she uttered. "I hope you feel better soon."

"I will M&M's," he replied, squeezing her body closer to him with great care not to tear his stitches. Rick had been calling Joyce "M&M's" since the day she was born.

"Me too, Daddy!" Victoria cried out from her seat at the table.

"Thank you, Pumpkin."

"Hey, Mommy," Victoria continued. Can me and Michael go outside to play on the swings for a little more? It's still light out and daddy can watch us from the window."

I looked at Rick. "It's fine by me. I'm just sitting here."

"Ok, guys," I said. "But the minute I call you in, you have to come."

It seemed that even before I finished my sentence, our two oldest kids had scurried out the door.

"What about me, Mommy?" Joyce yelled from where she stood next to Rick.

"You, Joycee, need a bath."

Walking over to her and picking her up, I traded Rick his cell phone for our adorable daughter. It had been vibrating incessantly throughout dinner. Now that dinner was over, Rick would answer it.

We had instilled a strict "no phone during dinner" policy early on in our marriage to ensure that "our relationship" didn't suffer at the hands of our business success...now it was "our family." Sometimes, like today, it was tough to stick to, as incessant as the prodding had been. We did it anyway, turning it off completely then placing it in the drawer until dinner was finished. It solved the issue completely, staving all potential distractions.

"Have fun M&M's," Rick said. Finding his voicemail icon, he began listening to the messages.

Joyce and I slipped from the room and returned some twenty minutes later, our daughter clean as a whistle and smelling like a rose. Holding her high in the air as to share our accomplishment and the new nightgown I had bought her, I looked at Rick then immediately lowered her back down.

His expression was like I'd never seen it before. I became instantly concerned, bordering on panic even. "Honey," I said. "Is everything Ok?"

He looked at me, struggling to answer but not knowing where to begin. "Evie, you need to put the kids to bed," he said, his voice shaking.

"Ok," I replied, responding to his reaction in the only way that I could.

I opened the door and called to the other children, "Michael,

Victoria, time to come in." Quickly, they ran, scrambling inside laughing freely...not a care in the world.

"I beat you," screamed Michael.

"It's not fair. You are bigger than me," Victoria shot back.

"And I always will be," Michael stated proudly.

Then directing them, somewhat sternly, I said, "Guys, go kiss your father and jump into your pajamas. It's time for bed."

"What do you mean, Mom?" Michael questioned. "It's still light out."

"I know, Michael," I answered. "Everybody is going to bed early tonight. Daddy and I are tired."

Rick motioned both the kids his way. He hugged each one of them tightly; the intensity of which characterized the monumental nature of the problem we needed to discuss. Then planting a kiss atop each of their heads, he sent Michael and Victoria over to me to put to bed. Ushering the kids down the hall, I turned back to Rick and mouthed, "Who was on the phone?"

Rick replied, "Asher."

My mind went into overdrive. Asher Cohen was Dr. Crohn's protégé. *What possible news could he have told Rick that has sent him into such a state?* I thought. *Whatever it was, we would face it together.*

I placed Joyce in her crib and motioned, "Night, night." Then reading Michael and Victoria a story, I tucked them into their beds as well. They quickly fell fast asleep, tired from the extra playtime outside.

Leaving the doors to their rooms open just a crack like usual, I lay my eyes on their innocent faces not knowing what was to come. With this in mind, I decided to shut their doors fully. It felt like it was the right thing to do, after all. Something inside me told me so. Thankfully, I listened.

Chapter 13

The Cancer

I stood in the hallway between the children's bedrooms for a moment, covering my face with my hands as if to force onto me a state of composure. I needed this prior to speaking with Rick. I knew that once I walked back into that kitchen, Rick would explain why Asher had been calling so aggressively. I wasn't quite sure that I was ready for that explanation but I couldn't leave Rick alone with the news any longer.

"Here you go," I said to myself, feeling as if I had just taken a seat at the mouth of a chute, moments prior to releasing my grip. I walked back down the hall and approached Rick with what I could only hope was a calming demeanor.

He seemed relieved when I finally returned. "Evie, come sit over here," he said, motioning to a spot on the couch right next to him.

I immediately did as he had asked. The weight of the impending news was growing heavier by the minute as was the struggle inside Rick. I could tell. It was obvious that he wanted to protect me, but it was even more obvious that he couldn't. The problem was just too big.

"Evie," he finally began. "Evie, Asher would like to see us both in his office at eight o'clock tomorrow morning. The lab results from my surgery came back this afternoon. I have cancer."

The voice inside me wailed in horror. Thrust into a state of confusion and panic, my mind began to race. *You're going to have to raise these kids alone just as your father did you,* I thought to myself. A well of tears filled my eyes, straining the composure I had previously pulled together. Rick leaned over to hug me.

"I don't understand!" I cried. "Asher told you that news over the phone? How is that possible?"

There was a piece of me that was hoping Rick was kidding, lessening the blow perhaps for some other bad news he needed to share. The odds of that happening, however, were slim.

Rick would never kid about something like this, especially knowing how hard I'd prayed to never hear those words again after my mother's death. *What kind of cruel joke was life playing on me and Rick...on our happiness...on our children? This can't be happening,* I thought, continuing to allow the news to sink in further. It was my worst nightmare come true.

"I forced Asher to tell me," Rick replied. "He was going to wait until tomorrow when he saw us, but I demanded that he tell me while we were on the phone." I nodded, knowing how Rick was especially in light of questionable news or in this case, really bad.

"Why should I think this would be any different?" I said to myself, finding some hope and comfort in that. Regardless, I began to sob. Thoughts of the kids, their innocence, and the impact the realities of this disease would have on both overtook me. I was frightened—frightened for them, me, and, mostly, Rick—not knowing what the future of our life together would be or if there would be one at all.

"You promised you'd never leave me. So many times...you promised," I was bawling uncontrollably now, remembering every time that Rick had said it as if by doing so this might alter reality.

"I'm not leaving you, Evie. Never in a million years. Not you. Not the kids. We will figure this thing out, you and me,...with Asher and Dr. Crohn's help too. We will. Don't lose hope," Rick continued stoically. "I need you to believe me."

Realizing how selfish I was behaving...how much worse this news was for Rick than me, I pulled myself back to my senses and told him that I believed him. I knew he needed this reassurance, "my confidence," in order to broach the battle ahead. Ultimately, he would be fighting for all of us. I had to do my part. I loved him. I didn't want to lose him. I was his wife and the vows that I had taken were "for better and for worse." *So what if today was "worse,"* I thought. As Rick said, "We would figure this out between us and the best medical team money could buy."

Embracing each other for some time thereafter on the couch, we allowed the news to sink in further, grateful for the untethered solitude afforded to us by our worn out children. Then, when we could no longer avoid exhaustion ourselves, I walked Rick to our bedroom. He climbed into bed and I followed.

Neither of us could sleep, though, despite our inarguable weariness. We became consumed by the unknown. Fits of worry coupled with an unpredictable future plagued us. It ate away at any drowsiness we might have felt earlier. Morning could not come fast enough. At the same time, a part of me wanted the clock to stop completely.

Suspecting the worst despite the reassurance I had previously given to Rick, I didn't want to face what my intuition kept telling me. *Rick's prognosis wouldn't be good...not at all.* I knew I needed to brace myself for that possibility and quickly. Our "one time" perfect life was about to change and it was up to me to keep it together, which meant keeping me together too.

I shut my eyes and accepted the restless hours ahead. No doubt, motherhood had trained me to cope with sleepless nights, but not for the reason causing this one nor the many others to come. It couldn't prepare me for "never sleeping soundly again." Little could, except pure will and obstinance. I became keenly adept in both, so much so, in fact, that I would eventually master the ability to exist mostly on cat-naps. They'd sustain me until I could afford myself longer pockets of rest, laid out in the calendar that kept me functioning with few hitches to speak of.

I found it fascinating how adaptable human beings were when they needed to be, including manufacturing a small "sense of control" where little *sense* or *control* remained. *No wonder our species has survived so long,* I thought to myself, as I realized the double-edged sword hidden within that statement. *We had the fittest among us to thank for this.* I prayed that Rick fell on the right side of that line.

Me? I no longer had an option.

Chapter 14
The Treatment

"Hey guys. Come on in."

Asher stood in the doorway of his office. His solemn expression heightening my apprehension, my thoughts immediately turned to Rick and the nervousness he must be feeling. I continued to hold his hand, exiting the waiting room and reseating myself in front of Asher's desk. Rick did the same.

Following behind, Asher took his chair and opened a file that he had been carrying with him when he greeted us. In it lay numerous images, pictures of Rick's stomach, small intestine and the surrounding areas. He turned the top image around so that we could both see clearly what Asher was about to explain.

"I'm sorry that Dr. Crohn couldn't be here instead of me," Asher began. "Unfortunately, he's in Israel and in light of the seriousness of the situation, he didn't want to wait until he came back to discuss this with you."

"That's Ok, Asher," Rick replied. "You and I have known each other for so long... it's just as easy hearing the news from you."

Asher sighed deeply. He became noticeably upset prompting my heart to begin to pound even harder.

"Asher," Rick said. "Just spill it."

I knew Rick couldn't take another minute of waiting. Neither could I.

Asher began. "Rick, As I mentioned over the phone yesterday, the specimen that the surgeon removed from you during surgery was full of cancer...a type of cancer that normally isn't found in this particular organ. What I didn't tell you is that the lab isn't quite sure if this cancer is the only cancer you have. You might have another one as well—both being quite rare."

I continued to sit silently, taking in the entire exchange and processing it as calmly as possible.

"So how do we find out?" Rick questioned, using an unexpectedly clinical tone for a man who had just been told something catastrophic about his own life. I, on the other hand, could feel my panic surfacing once again.

"We send the specimen to another lab, Memorial Sloan Kettering, and let them test it." Pausing, Asher heaved a deep sigh, then continued. "Rick. Evie. There is one more thing." Asher took his pen and began lightly circling a portion of the image. "You see this?"

Rick and I both nodded.

"This is cancer. Your cancer is no longer contained. In other words, your cancer has already metastasized. It's spread throughout your body. You are in the fourth stage, Rick." Asher fell quiet.

"I don't remember much after that," I said to Debra. "I believe the shock of the news somehow drowned out everything around me. It was as if no one else existed in the room and it remained that way until I felt a sudden pressing on my forearm. Rick was signaling me that it was time to leave."

The entire conversation was over. The only thing left to do now was to wait for the new lab results to come back then set up an appointment with Dr. Jacob Wisch, the oncologist Dr. Crohn believed was best suited to handle our particular case. Unfortunately, I knew that neither was going to tell me anything that I didn't already innately know. We'd find out the following day that Rick indeed had two cancers at the same time. It was confirmed.

We would eventually learn that the first of the two had been growing inside him for at least eight years already or so Memorial Sloan Kettering believed. The onset of the second cancer was a bit harder to determine. Treating both, simultaneously, required nothing less than a genius if Rick had any hope of surviving. Thankfully, Dr. Wisch happened to be one, making us even more grateful that Dr. Crohn had arranged for Rick to be in his care. The cancer however wasn't impressed by the credentials that hung on this talented man's wall.

In time, it would become harder and harder to treat, regardless. This didn't keep Dr. Wisch from doing all that he could for Rick nor the host of other experts we flew in from around the world to consult on his case in the form of one big, fat, and expensive think-tank. It was an unimaginable amount of brainpower in a single room, all gathered together to "come up" with the perfect plan to save Rick's life. Out of it came two absolutes, Rick's prognosis hadn't changed and *optimism* was essential for any and all success, even if that ultimately meant buying Rick just one more day. Keeping Rick hopeful needed to continue.

"That's how they do it today," Debra remarked. "The whole mind-body thing. I agree for the most part."

"I do too," I replied, "although I couldn't help but wonder, during many of the chemotherapy treatments in which I kept Rick company, if we could have avoided his cancer altogether had Rick agreed to the surgery Dr. Crohn proposed immediately following our trip to Jamaica. Given what we were explained by Asher and then Dr. Wisch, I suspect they might have caught it when it was just getting started."

"You might be right," Debra replied. "Did you ever mention this to Rick?"

"No, not once. What good would it have done to have him look backward? How would this have helped to keep him optimistic? I bore that guilt for the both of us. I should have pushed him more to get the surgery, sided with Dr. Crohn more forcefully. It's been my biggest regret ever since."

"Evie, you are not a doctor. You couldn't have known," Debra said, eager to bring comfort to the woman whom she was growing to respect more and more.

"I know I am not, Debra, I just decided that the best thing that I could do for Rick was to join Dr. Wisch in his efforts to keep Rick's spirits up. And for almost two years, it seemed to be working...well that, the chemo, and the love that Rick and I shared, including for our children. We, ultimately, were able to delay the inevitable for much longer than anyone could have ever anticipated. The flip side of this however resulted in a tremendous amount of extra pressure on me, of which I could say nothing about.

As each day passed, Rick grew in his denial. Because of this, I was left to face much of our reality alone. This included managing the children in a way that would cushion the inevitable. I had to prepare the kids for the loss of their father without him, just as I had to prepare myself, minus the practical conversations and intimate exchanges I'd wished we'd had. Doing so might have relieved some of the guilt that I'd continue to carry with me long after Rick had passed."

"Does this mean that the two of you never talked about the possibility of you remarrying?" Debra asked.

I shook my head up and down. "The sole time I broached the conversation, he refused to discuss it—still insisting that he wasn't going anywhere. I didn't have the heart to push the matter. I couldn't steal his hope from him, which is exactly what I would have been doing had I continued. The one person in the world who was supposed to believe in him, no longer did? I just couldn't do that to him. I just couldn't."

"You did the right thing, Evie," Debra said, consoling me. "You're a strong woman. No wonder your kids are all doing well. She glanced at their photos resting on the windowsill across the room.

"What did you do to keep yourself going?" she questioned. "I mean, with you taking care of everybody else, it must have been really hard. How did you keep it together?"

"Truthfully," I said. "I leaned on my faith...prayed a lot."

"I remember this one instance when I went to refill a prescription of Rick's at the pharmacy, only to be denied simply because of an insurance glitch. I had been talking with the woman standing behind me at the time. We had been sharing our stories, so she knew about Rick's illness and my desperate need for his medication. Enraged by the pharmacy technician's explanation, this woman took matters into her own hands. Her ruckus caused the pharmacist to refill Rick's prescription personally, coupled with an apology. I thanked the woman wholeheartedly.

She replied, "My pleasure. You would think that they'd know better. Where's God when you need him?"

My response was sudden and absolute, "In people like you, who step up to help others without being asked. That's where he is."

I made a "hardcore" friend that day. I also realized just how deep my faith had become, deeper than I could ever remember. I guess I needed it to be. I needed to turn to someone, especially during moments when I couldn't find any more strength of my own and didn't have Rick to lean on either. I didn't blame Rick for this. It was just asking too much of him. That's what God's for, I believe.

"Tough times will make you do that," Debra remarked.

"Ain't that the truth," I said, grabbing a cookie from the plate and taking a bite. I was getting hungry, having never intended for our conversation to last this long, but not minding that it had. I was glad Debra was getting to know me, and me her. It seemed befitting, given the situation and frankly, I liked her from the start.

"On the lighter side of things," I continued. "I took up running again. I bought myself a treadmill, parked it in the kids' playroom, and began running every morning. Doing so centered me and increased my ability to cope with the enormous amounts of stress I was regularly contending with. I also resumed drawing my Flumps, which led me to begin writing stories about them as well. The kids seemed to love them, making our bedtime ritual even more fun."

"Then there was my crocheting. I spent hours crocheting Rick a scarf, the length and style of which was based on one of his favorite sci-fi characters, Dr. Who. I worked on that thing for months, finishing just in time for winter, which was perfect because—with Rick losing his hair and all—he needed an extra-long scarf to wrap around him from head to toe."

"So, he did lose his hair?" Debra asked.

"Yes, he did. He even had the kids help him shave his head the minute it began to fall out. We thought it might ease the fear associated with seeing their father bald. It worked. They still remember that day fondly...all of them, that is, except Grace? She was just too young."

"Does Grace remember anything?" Debra questioned.

"No," I answered. "Not a thing which is a reality we recently had to cope with."

"How so?" Debra asked.

"I will get to that part in a bit," I answered.

"Alrighty then...potty break for me," Debra announced. "Mind if I use the bathroom?"

"Not at all. Do you need any help getting up or walking over there?" I asked, pointing in the direction of the powder room closest to the kitchen.

"Nope. You just sit tight. I will be back in a jiffy. I'm looking forward to hearing the rest of your story. Can you do me a favor, though?"

"Sure thing," I answered.

"Great," she said. "About thirty minutes shy of the ending, let me know so that I may call my ride back to the office."

"You didn't drive yourself?" I asked.

"No," she said. "I can't drive for another few weeks."

"Then I certainly will," I replied.

With that, Debra slipped behind the door, and I finished my cookie.

Chapter 15

The Goodbye

"Now, where were we?" Debra said, returning from the powder room. "By the way, was that a photo of Rick I saw in the bathroom with the kids?"

"Yes, it is," I said. "One of my favorites. I remember that day like it was yesterday. We had embarked on a sailing expedition with the children. They were excited. When we finally docked, we were in Narragansett. The setting was so breathtaking that I asked Rick to pose with all of them huddled around him while I snapped a picture. He scooped them up, bent down, and... well, there you have it. They all looked so happy."

"They absolutely do," replied Debra.

"He was newly sick then so he didn't show any real signs of his cancer at the time that photo was taken," I commented.

Debra returned to her seat and then continued, "When was it that your husband became "full-on" ill?"

"Right before we hit the three-year mark. Although it seemed that the chemotherapy regime that Dr. Wisch had placed Rick on had beaten back the faster growing of the two cancers, the deadlier one found a stubborn foothold. It forced Dr. Wisch to suddenly change gears and chemotherapies. The impact on Rick's health, my life, and our home was severe.

No longer capable of running the business at all, even from our bed, Rick asked his older brother David to step in. Knowing that David had never had any experience in this role before, I wasn't quite sure that Rick's decision was a good one. But I also realized that our circumstances required someone to take over, and I couldn't do it. Nor would I, believing that my time left with Rick was better served by his side.

We were running out of it. I could see the writing on the wall, even though Rick remained steadfast in his denial. "A temporary necessity," is what he called it when he turned over the reins to David. I let him believe whatever he wanted. *What did it matter?* I prayed that the employees would help David keep the company afloat. "If not," I said to myself, "I would pick up the pieces when I had to." I could do no more than that. My head needed to be on Rick and the moments we had left.

From that point on, Rick's and my life together transformed itself into a series of chemotherapy treatments, abbreviated periods at home, and drawn-out hospital stays, one of which, unexpectedly, rekindled our relationship with Baron. The gravity of the situation had obviously been weighing on Baron. He could no longer stay away and watch his son die from afar. I was glad for this and gave Baron a big hug when I saw him. He returned the gesture, asking how I'd been in the process. Observing this exchange made Rick extremely happy.

The rest of that afternoon was spent catching up on current events and chit-chatting about the children. I showed him recent photos of them on my phone. He seemed quite pleased. When it was time for him to finally depart from his visit, he told us that he would be back again. He gave Rick a warm hug and kiss and then asked me to step out into the hallway with him for a quick minute. I did so without hesitation. Once alone, Baron told me that he was so grateful that I had married Rick and that he had been a fool. He wanted to let me know that, if I or the children needed anything, to just ask.

"Thank you, Baron," I answered. "That means a lot to me."

Baron then made me promise to bring the kids up to the family home as soon as possible. I agreed. He left shortly thereafter, stopping only to grab a cup of coffee on his way out. He'd return a few days later as he had promised.

As time went on, I began relying more heavily on Estelle, Saul, Elliott, and Elizabeth to help me care for the children. The pace, stress, and physical demands I carried on my shoulders regularly became exhausting. I barely had time to eat which caused me to shed twenty-five pounds, literally, overnight.

Then there was the strain of watching Rick slowly die. It was almost too much for me to take. His skin turned a grayish hue. His features began to resemble that of an old man. Admittedly, I was struck by how closely Rick resembled his grandmother from the photos he had shown me of her in her later stages of life. I had never thought that before. Just another thing this ugly disease had changed my mind about.

Eventually, Rick would need surgery, allowing his body to function by bypassing certain organs that no longer could. The surgery seemed to breathe life back into him in a way that astounded all of us. For a period of time, Rick was able to return home and stay there for a few weeks with the assistance of Hospice.

I remember sitting at the kitchen table with the Hospice nurse.

She was a tall woman with an extremely compassionate face, the type you would expect to see on someone who worked in this field. As I began filling out the required paperwork that she had brought with her, she said something to me that I had no idea I needed to hear. Afterward, I felt relieved alongside a sense of guilt for doing so. It was wholly unexpected.

She said, "Evie, it won't get any harder than this. You are going through the roughest part now, believe me. People always think that "later" will be worse. That's just not so and something I try to help loved ones understand ahead of time...when I first meet them."

I broke down crying, extremely appreciative that she had had the forethought to tell me. Her kind words helped keep me holding on. When I looked back at that moment years later, I concluded that this woman's thoughtfulness was just another way that God was using people to help me survive the horror.

"Sounds like it," Debra answered.

"She also told me another thing," I said to Debra.

"What was that?" Debra asked.

"She told me not to overlook my upcoming birthday but to celebrate it, even if that meant having a small party at home with Rick and the kids. I had mentioned that it was right around the corner in a prior conversation, and she was concerned that I would allow it to pass without so much as a cake. She told me that ignoring it wouldn't be good for anyone, especially me, who could use a few moments of feeling special."

Had she not said that to me, she would have been right. I would have skipped my birthday entirely. Instead, I enlisted the kids to help me bake a cake, create party decorations, and pull together some other simple plans for the day. They were very excited at the prospect of throwing their mom a birthday party, and I was glad that the Hospice nurse, Joan, had suggested it. When the day arrived, however, before anyone had even blown up the first balloon, Elliott showed up unexpectedly.

"What are you doing here?" I asked as I opened the door and invited him in.

He responded, "Rick asked me to come. He told me that you guys are going out and that he needed me to help him make that happen. So here I am."

"What?" I replied. "How are we going out? He can barely stand."

"Evie, I have no idea what's in his head but I'm not about to say no."

"Rick," I called while walking into our bedroom. Elliott remained in the foyer and wrestled with the kids.

"Rick," I called a second time, no longer seeing him in our bed where I'd left him. He was in the bathroom struggling to get dressed. The bag that the surgeon had attached to his abdomen kept him from completing the task easily on his own. I continued, "Rick, Elliott is here. He says you asked him to come over because we are going out?"

"I did," Rick replied from a distance. "It's your birthday and I want to take you and the kids out for lunch...celebrate it properly."

"But Rick," I continued, "the kids already made me a party. They are waiting to share it with the both of us." Not wanting to point out the obvious, I blamed my hesitance on the children.

Rick replied, "We will have that party tonight, Evie. Right now, my love, we are going out. You might want to get dressed."

Having no idea what else to do, I told the older kids to get dressed too. I dressed Joyce and Grace, then dressed myself. By eleven-thirty in the morning, we were all ready.

Elliott helped us into his SUV and drove us over to the next town and the restaurant in which Rick had made reservations. It was a steakhouse I adored. We had spent many happy times there and I guess today, we would spend one more. Little did I know that waiting inside for me was an enormous party in honor of my birthday. Rick and Rachel had been in cahoots, I'd learn, coordinating the event completely under my nose. I nearly fell over when I walked in.

"Happy Birthday!" everybody screamed. Rick had rented out the entire place to celebrate his love for me in the most memorable of ways. Before the affair ended, he lifted his glass and toasted me using all of the strength that he had left to do so.

"Evie," he said. "You are the love of my life. I don't know what I would do without you. Happy Birthday, Sweetheart. I love you."

"I love you too, Rick," I cried, overwhelmed by how courageous my husband continued to be as well as the depth of love he still felt for me. Among all of the tough moments and the painful realities, one thing remained perfectly clear. I had been right to marry Rick, exceptionally right, and I would have done it again given the chance.

The chance never came. That birthday was the last birthday I would ever share with Rick. He entered the hospital a week later. The few days that followed were the worst of my life.

Rick began to lose his mind amid his body shutting down. I struggled with allowing the kids to see him one last time, knowing the importance of providing them with the opportunity to adequately say "goodbye."

After much prayer, I decided to bring them to the hospital. God gave them twenty minutes of pure joy together. He had had mercy on them all, making Rick the best that he could be until the children left to return home with Elliott. He only screwed up Michael's name once, calling him by his own father's name, Baron.

Michael seemed to barely notice as he led his sisters out of the hospital room in a big brother sorta way. Michael's maturity had obviously been evolving as his father's health was in decline. I noticed this more and more lately. "I guess that's natural," I said to myself as I watched the girls scurry out behind him followed by Elliott.

The only time I ever saw Rick break down in tears throughout his entire illness was in the minutes following the departure of the children that day. Rick realized that his thoughts were becoming fuzzy. Teardrops slid down his cheeks as he grew frustrated by his inability to think clearly any longer.

Dr. Wisch reacted by increasing the dosage of the sedative that he had already prescribed for Rick to cope with the emotional pain and anger. He did the same with the medication Rick needed to manage the agony associated with the physical deterioration of his body too. The cancer was voracious and unrelenting by now.

Rick fell into a state of unconsciousness from that point on. He didn't move...didn't blink an eye. His shallow breathing was the only indication that he was still alive. It was at this point that Dr. Wisch told me that "we were near the end." He recommended that I call everyone in the family to come to the hospital to say their farewells.

One-by-one they came, sharing words of comfort, encouragement and love to which Rick could not respond. My heart broke with each new visitor that arrived. I couldn't believe this was happening. Rachel became distraught. Estelle began to weep. I was glad that she had Saul to comfort her, so worried was I that she would collapse under the weight of watching her son die. Baron was the last to come and his parting words were the hardest to hear. He continued to stand outside Rick's hospital room for some time thereafter, offering himself to me as a means of strength and support. Eventually, it was just Elliott, me, Estelle, and Saul who remained.

I rested my weary body next to Rick on his bed, holding him. I couldn't help but remember the conversation we had had years prior on the boat—the one where he told me that he was going to cure death. How I once again wished that he had done so...that anyone had. First my mother...now Rick.

I couldn't imagine my life without him. I didn't even want to think about it. I was hoping that he could feel my love for him through my embrace. It was impossible for me to truly know, but I didn't want to stop even if he couldn't as I knew how precious these last moments together were. *I would never get them back again,* I kept thinking to myself.

When Dr. Wisch arrived to finally check on Rick, he found that the cancer had broken through Rick's stomach wall. It was ravaging Rick internally. No more stays would be granted. The time had finally come to collect upon what it had initially come for when it first appeared.

I hated it. Hated what it had done to us. And just when I thought that my hatred couldn't have escalated any more, Dr. Wisch informed me that the cancer had suddenly punctured through Rick's skin.

The news sickened me. The notion that nothing could be done to stop it, that the best physicians in the world couldn't simply enter Rick's body and rip the cancer out as aggressively as it had taken over, continued to stun me as irrational as that sounds. All that Dr. Wisch could do now was to swiftly call the nurses into the room to take care of the wound, temporarily. My wound, however, remained wide-open and leaking of disgust, shock, and sorrow.

After the nurses completed their task, I resumed my position next to Rick on the bed. It was at this moment that Dr. Wisch explained to me that he would need my permission to change Rick's painkillers to ones that could handle the amount of pain Rick was experiencing currently despite his inability to speak. He explained to me that my permission was needed at this point given the high probability that the dosage required could cause Rick to die. Dr. Wisch concluded by saying, "If it was my wife, I would do it."

I thought about the vow that I had made to Rick, promising to keep him alive at all costs, given this day ever came. I then looked at Estelle, hoping that she might offer me a clue as to what she wanted me to do in the situation as well. Her wishes came in the form of one clear, agony-filled nod. She wanted me to agree to the new painkillers, no longer able to watch her child suffer.

It was a dramatic change from the morning I told her that Rick needed to return to the hospital yet again. Sensing the gravity of the situation, Estelle lashed out at me, begging me not to bring him as Dr. Wisch had ordered me to do. She cautioned me that she believed that Rick would die this time if I brought him there, then continued by warning me "about living with myself" in the event that she was right.

It was the one and only time Estelle had ever been cruel to me. Her words felt like a sledgehammer to my head. But I understood them and the grief in which they came. Now she was imploring me to put Rick out of his misery. I weighed everything, devastated and struggling with a decision I didn't want to make.

My mind raced between facts and a single promise...back and forth, then back and forth again. I thought about the moment Rick and I had first met and all of the happy times since. I thought about the many challenges that we had faced together and overcome. I thought about how crazy in love with him I still was, even in the decrepit state in which he lay. And I thought about the kids, especially Michael, who would be losing his father at the same age that Rick had lost Baron, albeit under different circumstances. It was no doubt one of the reasons Rick had fought so hard to stay alive amid the odds. I left nothing uncovered in making my decision.

In the end, I gave Dr. Wisch my permission. In doing so, I felt like I wanted to die too. But I couldn't. I was the one being left-behind...the one now required to carry the torch for the two of us. It was a sobering thought at the center of the tragedy that was ensuing.

The nurse arrived in the room a few moments later. She injected the IV attached to Rick's arm with the fluid. I was the only one in the room with Rick, at the time, taking my last few moments with him to say goodbye.

I laid my head on his chest. I could hear his heart pumping not unlike the many times I had before, only this time it's rhythmic pounding sounded almost too consistent. I had no idea how I was going to live with myself after this...after he was gone, knowing how I'd broken my promise to him. I had no idea if he would have kept mine, given things were turned around. The only thing I knew was that I loved him, and like Estelle, I couldn't watch him suffer anymore.

Wiping the tears from my eyes as I continued to lay in silence next to him, I told Rick that "I loved him."

Rick lay motionless. Still, something inside me told me that he had heard me. He hung on for another few hours. It would take Estelle prodding me to tell Rick that "the children and I would be fine without him" for him to finally let go. She was convinced that he was fighting his death for fear of leaving us behind. Ultimately she seemed to have been right. Moments after I whispered to Rick the reassurance that he required, he died. The life that had once occupied his ragged body was no more. And with it, left my heart.

Chapter 16

The Funeral

Sitting in a small lounge area writing the words to Rick's obituary couldn't have been more excruciating for me. I knew that the hospital morgue would soon be coming to Rick's room to take his body away, and I couldn't bear to witness this. It was enough that I had already observed the hollowness of Rick's corpse in the aftermath of his death. I felt raw inside. The finality of what had just occurred was settling in. I couldn't handle the blaring exclamation point that this necessary reality would place on his passing too.

No one could have prepared me for any of this, including the task at hand. I kept thinking to myself, "How do I capture this incredibly unique and loving human being's life in a few short paragraphs to do him justice—my beautiful husband and the father to my children?"

The tragic end of a good man who had brought so much meaning to my world seemed so senseless and unfair. Nothing I wrote would change that nor the grim job ahead of having to tell the children. My thoughts flashed back to a story the Rabbi once told me about the loss of his own father at a very young age.

His mother, for fear of what the news would do to him, kept his father's unexpected death secret for over two years prior to finally telling him. She just didn't know what to say or how to say it. Worried about the impact it would have on her son at the time, she decided not to say anything at all. Eventually, the excuses she made throughout his father's absence would wear thin. "The implications of withholding that news ended up being far worse for the Rabbi than had she told him the truth to begin with," the Rabbi had said.

I never understood why the Rabbi had shared that story with me at the time that he did. Maybe he was just venting. Maybe he had some sort of inkling of what was to come without realizing it. Either way, I understood his mother's decision intimately now. Less harsh was my judgment of her with regards. The position I presently found myself in brought me no closer to agreeing with her on the matter but sympathetic, I became. Telling the kids that their father was dead would not be easy in the least.

I looked at the pen that I had grabbed from my purse upon sitting down. The name "Remington" was inscribed across one side. It was a duplicate of the pen Rick had handed me when we first met. They were common to my life now but the irony at this particular moment added to my overwhelming remorse.

Saul came into the lounge hoping to bring me comfort but I couldn't accept his kind gesture quite yet. Instead, I snapped at him, intentionally driving him away until the scribble that he had asked me to put down on paper was done. I would one day apologize for this behavior but "today" wasn't that day. At thirty-five years old, I was a widow...responsible for raising our four children alone...to provide, protect, and love them without Rick. What a bitter fate to have to stomach.

I felt numb. It was a feeling that would remain until I handed Saul back the sheet of paper and completed organizing the arrangements to release Rick's body to the funeral home. I would then leave the hospital for good, never again having to wind my way through the corridors to find Rick. I knew where he was, and it wasn't a place he deserved to be...not at his young age nor without me.

It was early morning when the kids greeted me with an exuberance that matched my abnormally long disappearance to the hospital. Elizabeth had been watching them during the time that I had been away and was holding Grace in her arms on the couch when I walked in. Victoria and Joyce rushed to the door when they heard the bustle of me making my way inside.

I grabbed them simultaneously and gave them a big squeezy hug. Michael stood still in the background—his anxious expression already telling me that he knew. Releasing the girls, I walked over to Michael and pulled him close. He began to wail. Redness and tears overcame him, startling the girls and coercing Victoria to immediately ask what's wrong?

"Is it Daddy?" she asked. "Is Daddy dead?"

Still holding Michael, I turned to face the rest. Then squatting down to eye level replied, "Yes, Victoria. Daddy has gone to heaven."

"Oh," she said. "I'm going to miss him."

"Me too," I replied.

"Does he hurt anymore?" Victoria continued.

"No, Sweetie. Daddy doesn't hurt anymore," I answered, struggling to control my tears as I tried to bring some understanding to a situation that I couldn't understand myself.

"That's good," she said. "I'm still going to miss him."

"We all are, Pumpkin," I replied. "But he is still here. We just can't see him because he's sitting next to God now. God didn't want daddy to be in pain anymore so he fixed it so that he wouldn't be. He hasn't left us though. He's just in a different place watching over us now."

"I understand," answered Victoria. Then looking at her sister who had been intently listening in, Victoria cried, "Hey Joyce. Let's go play in my room." A minute later, they were scurrying down the hall and were gone.

Elizabeth sat in astonishment clutching Grace and searching her thoughts for the right thing to say, but there was no right thing. She settled on, "I'm so sorry, Evie. Whatever I can do for you and the kids, just let me know. I am here for as long as you need me."

I responded with a gracious smile then asked if she would stay with us through the evening. I needed her help especially as the funeral was just two days away, not a lot of time to prepare. As Jewish law dictated that the dead needed to be buried as quickly as possible, adhering to it was critically important to me. I had already failed to keep my promise to Rick once—something I wasn't quite sure I'd ever be able to get over as it was. "A problem for another time," I decided.

Leading Michael into the kitchen, I wet a paper towel with cool water to wipe his face. Then taking my usual seat at the end of the table, I placed him in his chair next to me. I handed him the paper towel and began to talk.

That was the day Michael and I became a team, a team that would eventually include all of the children. I adopted an old-fashioned parenting model, where my older children were expected to take care of the younger ones. All of the kids were expected to help out. Each answered to the other and, in turn, they all answered to me. The reason behind was "pure love"...love for Rick and love for the benefits a close-knit family would provide. Ours was made up of five people now, five pieces to a legacy we all wanted to honor. We took that seriously.

"I think we should light a candle every night at dinner in honor of daddy so that it feels like he is joining us at the table," I said to Michael. "What do you think?"

Michael shook his head in agreement then asked, "Mom, what is the funeral going to be like?"

Michael, being so young, had never been to a funeral. How sad to think that the first one that he would ever attend would be his own father's.

"Well, Michael," I said. "There will be lots of people. The Rabbi and the Cantor from our temple will be there to say a few prayers. Some of us will be speaking about Daddy to those who attend, remembering all the good things about him. Then at the end of everything, a few of Daddy's brothers and friends will carry daddy's casket out to the hearse where they will place it inside. Thereafter, all of us will drive over to the cemetery where a few more words will be said and then daddy will be buried. Following that, lots of people will come over to our house to stay and eat for a bit. That will begin our Shiva period. Sound Ok?" I asked.

"Yes," Michael replied. "But Mom," he continued quite out of the blue. "Can only my uncles and Daddy's friends carry his casket or can I carry it too?"

Stunned and disbelieving that I had just been asked that question by my young son about his father, I thought deeply and quickly about my answer. Aware that I needed to meet the needs of Michael in every situation, notwithstanding this one, I replied, "Michael, you can carry the casket too. But if at any point in time, and I mean ANY, you decide that you can't go through with it, just tell me and we will find a replacement." I didn't want to lock Michael into something that he might not ultimately be prepared to do, all good intentions aside. At the same time, I did not want to deny him.

"I promise," he said, a statement followed closely behind by a second request, this time to speak at the funeral. I agreed under the same conditions which seemed to ease any outstanding worry Michael might have had with regards to his role in the funeral.

The kids, me, and Elizabeth spent the rest of the day huddled together in a manner of speaking. The abnormal nature of our current circumstances seemed to temporarily fade for all of them as we watched television, played outside, and ate both lunch and dinner. I tried everything to keep it together during this time, pulling back pools of tears and choking rage that crept up on me without warning. I hid them well...from everyone but me. Thankfully, Saul had taken charge of handling all of the details for the funeral. I was, again, grateful.

When night finally arrived, Elizabeth and I helped each other tuck the children into their beds. Then wrapping me up in a comforting embrace, Elizabeth left for the evening, leaving me to survive the night alone. "Let me know if you would like me to come back tomorrow," she said as she closed the door behind her. "I'd be happy to."

"Thank you, Elizabeth," I said. "I think I will be Ok for tomorrow."

"Then, I will go to the office," she said, pausing to see if I was going to permit her to tell everyone there that Rick had passed.

"Elizabeth," I responded. "Could you please share the news with the rest? I'm not up to that right now and I'm not sure David is either. I doubt he's even going in tomorrow."

"Certainly," she said. Then off she went, leaving me completely alone with the most crippling ache that I had ever felt in my life.

The rest of the night was torture. I could not sleep. Curled up on my side of the bed, wearing Rick's sailing sweatshirt and weeping uncontrollably, I couldn't believe that I was here alone in the room in which we had slept together for so many years while he was lying on a cold slab in the morgue at the funeral home being watched over by an attendant we had hired to care for his body. I could hardly envision it nor did I want to.

I began to shiver despite the warmth and comfort of Rick's sweatshirt and the covers I had pulled over me. Struggling to succumb to the hardened reality of a life without him and what that meant, I screamed into my pillow with a ferocity that nearly made me pass out. "You were not supposed to leave me!"

That first scream led to another and then another until my unbridled anger eventually relented, replaced by an inescapable exhaustion that left me feeling weak and vulnerable. I closed my eyes and began praying, placing this night and all others in hands other than my own.

I immediately felt a peaceful sensation wash over me, as if two arms had just wrapped me up in an effort to take the pain away. I had no strength left to fight. I wanted to imagine that these arms were that of Rick's. I didn't care if this seemed crazy. I needed this. I needed to believe it at that moment. So I did. Shortly thereafter I drifted off to sleep—the first of many times I would do so in this way.

Two days later the funeral went off without a hitch. Saul, being Saul, had made sure to leave nothing to chance. There were lots of tears, wonderful eulogies, and yes, even Michael—the mature young man that he had grown into quite suddenly—stood tall in the face of his grief.

The kids and I, less Grace, threw dirt upon Rick's casket at the cemetery. A week later Shiva was over.

It wasn't long before everyone else's world went back to spinning again, except ours. Ours took more time to restart. When it did, however, I adopted an undeniably protective stance over my family, placing myself behind the needs of my children "routinely." This included arranging for a trust to be set up for their future as well as making sure that no one ever came between them and me.

It was a decision not always popular with some family members, school officials, and coaches but in the end, it proved to be the right one. The children would go on to flourish as would the bonds we reconstructed. We'd ultimately grow together and in many ways, grow-up together. This included me. I was still so incredibly young. When I look at old photos from back then, I marvel at how young. I didn't even realize it myself.

"There were so many obstacles to contend with," I said to Debra.

"I can't even imagine," she replied.

"No, you can't," I agreed. I said it with conviction. "What I went through after that? Honestly, you just can't make this stuff up."

"Then you best keep talking, my dear. You have me on the edge of my seat. By the way, may I have a tad-bit more tea?"

"Sure," I answered. "Let me just warm up another kettle of water."

"Perfect," she said. "In the meantime, I'll just jot down a few more notes."

"Nothing bad I hope?" I remarked.

"Not at all. Evie, you're a saint," Debra replied.

"I know some people who would not agree with you," I retorted.

"I'd be more worried if there weren't," responded Debra. "No one is liked by everybody. And what you went through didn't leave you a lot of room to be a *people pleaser*."

I smiled again. Pushing the teapot aside, I brought the kettle of hot water back to the table with two fresh tea bags and resumed where I had left off. The details poured out of me as readily as the newly brewed liquid to the thirsty cups. Where one was meant to soothe, however, the other continued to remain stirred.

Chapter 17

The Struggle

I spent most of the first year following Rick's death in overdrive, reframing our lives and keeping pace as I figured out how to do everything by myself. The newness of being a single parent held many surprises. I'd come to believe that all of them were devised to hone my ability to handle just about anything on my own without becoming flustered. All of this left me very little time to grieve. My most immediate concerns centered around ensuring that my children remained positive about life and their future as well as providing them with all of the love, security, and financial means required by both.

I have always been of the mind that the unpredictable, challenging circumstances thrust upon parents from time-to-time shouldn't be allowed to interfere with the overall welfare of their kids whenever possible. For me, this included Rick's death and indicated the line I now needed to tow alone to live up to this belief.

I adopted a "no excuse" policy for myself and, after a reasonable period of grieving, did so for the children as well. None of us were allowed to feel sorry for ourselves nor use Rick's death as an excuse to fail. Squandering life wasn't an option. "It was a privilege," I'd explain, "one daddy would want back again if he could." The realization that we were Rick's legacy and what that meant became part of our regular conversation.

There was only one instance that threatened to change our family's course in this regard. It happened a few months following Rick's death. Michael began to act out in school. He was being bold with his teacher, interrupting the class, and refusing to listen

When Mrs. Burke called me to discuss Michael's behavior, I was mortified, upset, angry, and worried. I told her that I would take care of it and that I would work with her to make things right.

When Michael returned home that day, I asked him and his sisters to join me in the car. I told them that *we were going to take a little drive—an outing of sorts.* They were all excited. Michael hopped into the front seat next to me, saying little about his day and nothing about what Mrs. Burke had shared with me. The girls chattered in the back and Grace quickly fell asleep in her car seat.

"Michael, I began," signaling the rest to quiet down. "Michael, your teacher called me today with some very disappointing news."

"She did?" Michael remarked in an agitated tone.

"Yes, she did." Michael remained silent so I continued. "She told me that you refuse to listen to her, that you are cutting up in class, and gloating about watching copious amounts of television as opposed to studying and doing your homework." By this time I had crossed the George Washington Bridge; my anger was becoming more apparent.

I entered Harlem and found a parking spot right next to some garbage cans that were piled high with bags of trash. The area was dirty and frightening, something Michael and the girls had never seen before. Their bewildered expressions were growing. I continued.

"Michael, your father and I have worked extremely hard to give you a good life, to send you to a great school and to make sure that you had, and have, everything you need to go to college and graduate. We placed the world at your fingertips. The only thing we ever asked from you in return was to be a respectful son, who tries hard in his studies." I paused then went on. "Well, Michael, according to your teacher, you are doing none of this, in fact, quite the opposite. So...look around you, Michael. Take a good look. Here is where you could end up if things don't change—a slum."

Michael looked around then turned back to me. He seemed unimpressed.

Suddenly, I pointed to the door opposite mine and in a booming voice yelled, "Get out!"

"What?" he screamed, completely panic-stricken over my command.

"Get out, Michael," I shot back. "If you are not going to take me or school seriously then you won't be going to college. I might as well save myself the aggravation and money as well as both of us the time and cut your trip short! It seems you really don't care. So...get out!!!"

Michael screamed again in terror, "No, Mommy, no." The girls chimed in as well, paralyzed by the notion that their brother could be living on the streets as opposed to in our home after today.

"Mommy, please don't make him!"

I looked at Michael, then at the girls, and then back at Michael and said, "Michael, if you don't want to stay here, you had better promise me that you will go back to working hard. You must also apologize to Mrs. Burke and listen to whatever that lady tells you to do. She is now in charge of your television time and everything else impacting your education until I say otherwise. Do you understand me?"

"Yes, Mommy. I do," Michael answered, still praying that he would remain in his seat and not sitting at the side of the curb, never to see or hear from any of us again.

"Good," I replied, turning the engine back on and driving Michael, his sisters, and me home.

No doubt many psychologists would have taken issue with my method to regain control over Michael and, indirectly, his sisters. Deep down, however, I didn't care. I needed to re-establish who was in charge and what to expect going forward. The "Harlem Run," as we would later call it, was undoubtedly the quickest way to do this in my opinion. And since I was the only adult raising them presently, my opinion was the only one that mattered.

I never again had an issue with Michael nor his sisters when it came to school after that day. Other things, yes. They weren't perfect kids nor was I a perfect mother, but our "team" mindset had returned. Any eventual hiccups couldn't hold a candle to the pride I felt for them as we continued on.

Being both mom and *dad*, to the degree that I could, became a labor of love not easily described. I sum it up in the form of a response that I gave to a stranger upon making the following comment to me in relation to Rick's death. She said, "You poor thing... your husband's gone and *you*, with all those kids."

I replied, "Thank God for all those kids." I couldn't imagine my life without any of them or the extraordinary piece of Rick that he had left behind. Maybe to some, our kids would have been a burden. To me, they never were.

Chapter 18

The Company

As the first series of holidays without Rick approached us, the pain of not having him there grew intolerable. The idea of lighting the Menorah or decorating the Christmas tree alone was impossible to think about without crying every time. I wasn't good at putting my emotions aside as Rick had been. I realized that I needed to get better at that. The holidays just wouldn't cooperate, however, especially as I could feel Rick's presence in every room.

Sometimes I even thought that I could see him—sitting in a chair in the family room, watching me as I ran on my treadmill or while I lay holding one of our girls in our bed at night during a bad storm. "Missing him" became even more pronounced during this time of the year.

This reality was further magnified by Estelle's inability to participate in our lives for much too long. So grief-stricken had she become by the loss of Rick, that she remained hidden since. She could face no one but especially me or her grandkids. She would eventually come around. An emotional plea from me coupled with a bit more time made sure of it.

To get through the season initially as a result, I decided to adopt a new tradition, one we would follow during the winter holidays every year thereafter. The children and I would spend Hanukkah and Christmas at home, and then on the morning of the twenty-seventh of December, we would travel somewhere that we had never been before and remain there through January 1st. We would ring in the New Year with each other among hundreds of other guests doing the same.

The kids and I would come to love these trips, eagerly awaiting the adventure and fun that they held. I knew Rick would have relished seeing the joy in his children's eyes and mine too. "He'd be beaming," I'd say to myself as the children sat patiently in the airport, anticipating the fun ahead and how amazing the airplane food would ultimately taste by 'kid' standards.

I had arranged our first adventure of this kind to be spent in Arizona. I had never been there before but it was an easy flight and seemed to hold everything young kids could want, including horses, hot air balloons, and jeep treks through the desert. I was looking forward to some time at the spa too. My body and mind weary, I was grateful the resort also offered a kids club in which to make that happen.

Moments prior to boarding the plane to Scottsdale, I decided to take the girls to the restroom. Michael didn't have to pee so he remained in his seat with strict orders not to go anywhere. I had already decided that the only way I could manage the trip safely was to place all three of my daughters on leashes so that I might not lose them while in the airport. I held tight to the three looped ends as they ran excitedly down the corridor towards the sign displaying the "little woman with the cute skirt" as Joyce called her. Joyce always loved to wear skirts. She felt extra special in this regard knowing that airports had signs celebrating this.

Passing by two women as the girls anxiously found their way inside the restroom with me dragging behind, I directed them to the handicapped stall and ushered them and me inside together. Each of my daughters took turns urinating. When it finally came time for me to do the same, I sat down on the toilet. The momentary pause gave me space to overhear a discussion taking place in the waiting area of the restroom. It centered upon "the cruel passerby who held her children on leashes like dogs." I couldn't believe my ears.

I was dumbstruck and angered all at the same time, having felt wrongfully judged for an act that seemed extremely humane. Rather than allow my children to get lost or be taken by some predator, I had decided to place my younger ones on leashes. Now I was being judged for it.

Wiping myself, then flushing, I opened the latch to the stall and guided my daughters over to the sinks to wash their hands. My glance towards my two critics along the way said it all. They looked down in embarrassment. It was at that particular instant that I gave up on ever caring what people thought of me again. Their insensitive comment wrapped a hard shell around me from that day forward, rebuking public scrutiny or any scrutiny at all. My decision would serve me well through the years.

Collecting Michael and my carry-on, the children and I boarded the plane. The smooth flight gave way to views of majestic mountains and endless tan sand. The kids couldn't wait for the plane to land nor to scramble into the car that I had arranged to take us to Canyon Ranch Resort. Then they couldn't wait to get out of it. When we arrived through the impressive gates, the grandness of the sites we came upon overshadowed all expectations.

The kids marveled at how beautiful Canyon Ranch was, including the towering Christmas tree in the lobby. It was just the beginning, we'd come to find out. There was so much to do, so much to see and so much to enjoy. We played, took tours, swam, and slept in late...or I tried to anyway when the kids would let me. By the time January 1st rolled around, none of us wanted to leave. The only thing that made it a bit easier was the realization that each holiday going forward held the same kind of fun and adventure. It was one of those new traditions that nourished us. Even so... for me, the flight home remained a long one, much longer than the flight that had allowed us to explore a whole new side of the country.

The fact of the matter was, I would begin assuming Rick's role at the company the week following our return and my nerves were getting the better of me. Trading my stay-at-home role for one as CEO and President wasn't exactly what I had ever wanted nor bargained for but, reality spoke that I needed to—for the sake of the company, the employees, the kids' college funds, and our livelihood. The pay-out from Rick's life insurance policy only covered a portion of Rick's medical bills. I still had some left to handle and I wanted to do that as quickly as possible so that I could begin building towards our financial future.

Being in debt was a concept never comfortable to me, nor Rick. So getting myself out of it was my first order of business. Everything that Rick had taught me about money and his work would now come into play. That said, nothing could have ever prepared me for the mess I'd be walking into when I did...absolutely nothing at all.

It took me about a week to put all of the pieces together.

Lengthy conversations, spreadsheets, and projections combined with phone calls with the corporate accountant and attorney unearthed a very grim picture. Rick's business was hemorrhaging. David had not only been incapable of laying the concerns of our anxiety-ridden clients to rest but he had failed to cultivate any new opportunities as well. Additionally, employee relations were extremely poor. A few were carrying the weight of the many, inspiring enormous resentment between. It was obvious that the company was literally on its last legs, a feeling I had become quite familiar with since Rick's illness began. Like then, I refused to give up.

Replacing David on the spot, I began to reorganize the entire company which included firing many. My aggressive measures sent a clear message to the remaining employees that things were about to change. "Free rides" would no longer be tolerated. The ripple effect was huge, notwithstanding David, who left angrily and did not speak to me for years thereafter. Some employees revolted. Others remained silent and began to vigorously pitch in. Many inherited an array of new titles unusual to them.

Increased workloads were coupled with a commitment to help me move the company back on track. This included preventing a rather unexpected hostile takeover, the threat of which was both terrifying and infuriating. We came through it well, but it left an impression on me as to how nasty "business" could actually become. I'd never forget that lesson.

The entire time we were navigating our way through, I kept asking myself, "What would Rick do? What would Rick do?" Somehow, the right answers always came. I found myself wondering if that was actually Rick's hand or my own. In the end, however, we survived, putting our aggressor out-of-business in the process. It was the beginning of a very unique time at the company.

My newly formed team was forced to stretch continuously. This included me as I waffled between "feeling completely unprepared and feeling totally confident," with a lot of dumb luck in between. Thoughts of *divine intervention or that of Rick's help* kept gnawing at me. Either way, what we did do, we did well, which would eventually include the addition of new products and services to our existing offerings and a total repositioning of the company. My one and only turnaround had been a success and in that, everyone was thrilled.

I was especially happy and relieved. The idea of losing what Rick and I had built together was terrifying to me...more terrifying than all of the demons that I needed to face to keep it alive. I wasn't ready to let the last remnants of Rick go, and as I couldn't save him, I'd be damned if I wasn't going to save his company.

That major career accomplishment would lay the groundwork for many others. None of them however would replace the emptiness I continued to feel without Rick. I just couldn't shake it. The pain of missing him wouldn't relent...and neither would the connection I still felt with him.

The passing of time wouldn't make a difference nor any form of therapy I underwent. And certainly re-entering the dating world wasn't the answer. It seemed to compound the problem, even more. Our bond remained steadfast despite all efforts to the contrary. Nothing seemed to be able to break it, leading me to believe that there might be more to my sensing, and even seeing, of Rick than I originally believed.

Having been able to communicate with a spirit once already, had I been unknowingly doing the same with Rick and Rick with me? I wasn't quite sure, but my frustration was growing. *How much longer would I live in this emotional purgatory?* I thought to myself.

I decided, for all our sake, that I needed to begin to actively break the ties that bound me to Rick. I ached for a new lease on life as "Evie," not Rick's wife, just "Evie." Who she was or what that meant, I had yet to find out but I was ready...especially knowing just how unpredictable tomorrow could be. "Time" wasn't going to wait for me to feel whole again nor offer me the perfect moment to begin. Rick's cancer had taught me that.

"Sounds like a smart decision," Debra remarked.

"Yes," I replied. "It was for the most part. Many of the choices I made from that point on truly improved mine and the children's lives. But as much as I sound like a phoenix rising from her ashes, don't be fooled. I stumbled as well. Frankly, I face-planted, admittedly. One particular incident went awry and took me with it. "

"Really?" Debra questioned.

"Really," I answered. "Thankfully, everything turned out alright in the end, but it took whatever I had left in me after losing Rick and saving the business to make it so. It was, ultimately, the main reason that I permanently moved here."

"You don't say," Debra replied. Then it had some good in it after all. I'm certainly glad you made that choice. And anyway...I've always believed that there is a reason for everything."

"Me too and it had a lot of good in it," I said. "I would have just preferred a different route to uncover it, honestly. That beautiful little boy that I got out of it, though, made it all worthwhile." I smiled at the photo of my youngest and fifth child taped to the door of the refrigerator.

"He sure is cute," Debra commented. "How old is he?"

"He's six and is the easiest kid you will ever meet."

"Seems it from the looks of him," Debra agreed. "So what actually happened?"

"We will get to that part. There are just a few other things prior to this that I need to explain first."

"Well then, let's do it," Debra blurted out. "Your life is better than any soap opera I've ever watched."

"Debra, I'm not quite sure that's a compliment, but thank you," I replied, taking another sip of tea from my teacup while thinking about the next part of my story. "It's been quite a journey for sure."

Chapter 19

The Vacation

"Come on, kids! Let's get into the car," I called. "We have to go."

It was Fourth of July weekend, and I had planned a getaway to Connecticut for the children and me to enjoy. We had not been there since Rick sold our sailboat during the second year of his illness. There had been no sense in keeping it. We couldn't use it and the expense of allowing it to sit in dry dock indefinitely was just too substantial.

It made me sad to think that the kids may never remember or even know what it was like to spend time traipsing around New England like sailing vagabonds. Rick had grown up on the water and this joy was something he'd really wanted to share with our children like he had done with me. This trip was my attempt to do that for him.

The place we were staying had been around for years. Rick and I would pass it on the way to the marina all the time. "Funny how we never thought to go inside," I said to myself as I locked Grace into her car seat beside Victoria. Michael was the last to hop in, taking the seat in front of Joyce's booster. Once fully buckled, we were off.

We spent most of the long ride listening to a variety of music—some pop, some country—and singing. Grace slept much of the way helping to ease the strain of the difficult traffic that delayed our arrival. When we finally made it, none of us could wait to get out of the car. Hunger had set in and everyone was famished.

"Hey, guys," I said to the kids. "Why don't I check us in quickly then we can change into our bathing suits and eat lunch at the pool?"

"Sure Mommy," Victoria screamed, peering out the window at all the fun the other kids were having in the water.

Before we knew it, we were there too—the kids in their goggles, sunhats, and flip flops and me with legs dangling over the edge of the kiddie pool holding Grace upright in the water. My focus shifted fanatically between Joyce, Victoria and Michael frolicking about in the adult pool. *How Rick would have loved to see this*, I thought, imagining his face filled with pride.

Without warning, I began to sense that Rick was sitting next to me, watching everything. "Evie, you've got to stop this," I said to myself. "Rick's gone and he's not coming back. This time is meant for you and the kids as much as it is to share with them more about their father."

"Very true," I answered myself.

We spent the rest of the afternoon enjoying the sunshine and fun. I had promised the children that we would eat dinner at a very special restaurant, one with a singing bridge. The image boosted their excitement to an entirely new level. When I finally called them out of the pool to get cleaned up and dressed, they bounced out without a complaint. An hour later we were in the car heading to Bill's Seafood.

Bill's was iconic in the area, well-known for their hot lobster rolls, loud music, and cash-only policy. Every boater knew it and ate there. It was a goldmine, to say the least. No one balked about the long lines and slow service during the summer as both were expected due to the joint's popularity. You never left Bill's without having had a good time...or hungry, for that matter.

Once we finally made it to the hostess stand, we were ushered to a table on the patio near the water. We ordered a ton of food, all of which included lots of fries, half of them going to the ducks paddling beneath the singing bridge. The children were having a glorious time and I was also, just being there with them. It was amazing how so much of mine and Rick's romance had been tied up in this place. The gratitude that I felt in being able to share it with the kids was indescribable.

By the time we returned to the hotel again, the children were exhausted. They fell asleep without even so much as a story. The plan for tomorrow was to take them to see Mystic Seaport and spend the day there. A good night's rest was in order. It was a plan that would turn out a bit differently than anticipated—one that would change the way we spent most weekends and holiday vacations thereafter. We bought a house.

Chapter 20

The Cottage

I hadn't expected to do it, but somehow, the idea of giving my children a little bit of "Mayberry" swept me away. It happened about ten minutes into our drive to Mystic Seaport. A realtor's sign suddenly caught my eye and so I followed it. I told the kids that it was part of our day's adventure. We landed at a cottage located on a nature preserve overlooking an inlet that flowed from the sound.

It was a tiny place laced with charm. An enormous apple tree stood tall in the front yard. I parked the car and immediately got out. The beauty of my surroundings compelled me to climb the stairs and knock on the door. Seconds later the door opened. An older gentleman greeted me. He was later joined by his wife.

I spoke. "Hi, there. My name is Evie Remington, and I am interested in learning more about your house."

The couple was very kind and told me as much as they could without involving the realtor. They even toured me around the yard of the home. My kids, now fully engaged, followed closely behind. At the end of it all, I asked the price and for the number of the realtor. Then thanking them, I placed everyone back inside the car and dialed the digits on the card that they had handed me.

One ice cream stop later—as to give the realtor a bit of time to drive over to the home—the kids and I viewed the interior. I made an offer that afternoon. We settled on a price by the end of the week, which included all of the furniture and an agreement to close in another two.

It was a decision that would ultimately become one of the best I'd ever made. That little house captivated every one of us. It dramatically assisted in our continued growth as a family, and it brought along with it a community of new friends, happy times, and memories that we would come to cherish—not only for Michael, Victoria, Joyce and Grace but for their little brother, Andrew, too.

I would later learn that the couple who had sold the cottage to me did so to cover expensive cancer treatments needed by the husband, the nice gentleman who had greeted me at the door. *Ironic,* I thought to myself when I learned of the news. It made me wish I'd paid them even more for the house as opposed to having negotiated as Rick had taught me.

"There's no going back," I reminded myself. "Just say a prayer for him and enjoy your family's time there as he had done with his." I knew this was the right way to think, the only way really given the unique circumstances that brought us together.

The kids and I loved our weekends nestled in the cottage. We'd watch movies, bowl at the local alley, browse the farmer's market, play miniature golf, relax on the beach, and chow down on some great food at Luigi's Restaurant when we wanted Italian over seafood. It seemed at one point as if we were eating at Luigi's every Saturday night.

The children loved the enormous dishes of fettuccine alfredo in which they split between them as well as the warm and homey atmosphere the owners provided. Those who ate there frequently were on a "first name" basis with the staff. We were included in that group. Beyond the sheer enjoyment of these meals was the ridiculously cheap price tag. I spent forty dollars to feed my entire family each time, with leftovers to spare. They would eat them for breakfast the following morning. The arguments over who "got more" were commonplace and frankly, made me feel good. Simple reminders that I was "doing a *good* job or *good enough*" on my own were appreciated. I relished them, in fact.

Our community of neighbors made it even more special for us. We grew close with many of them. The kids romped with the older boys next door who were more than happy to teach them the ropes. That family had owned their home for generations so they knew these ropes well. This was not unusual for many of the residents, we'd come to realize. Multi-generational homes were quite common. I hoped our family would eventually follow suit.

My favorite neighbors in the community were an older couple and their daughter. The Clarks adopted us, so to speak, from the moment they met me and the kids. They'd take the kids out for meals, spend hours chatting with me over cups of coffee and snacks, and text me ahead of time if there was dangerous weather to contend with during my three-hour drive from New Jersey to the cottage. I grew to love these people like my own family and in some ways, they became my family.

I also grew to love mornings on the back porch overlooking the nature preserve. My cup of coffee on the table near the outdoor couch, I relished watching the herons dance while the long grass swayed in the marsh behind the rickety old fence...the one I'd eventually have repaired. The view calmed me, putting me back together after a full week of juggling.

I'd ultimately decide to name our three-bedroom oasis "Flumpstown," after the town that I'd created in the collection of stories I'd written for the children. By now, "The Flumps" had become much more than simple drawings paired with clever words. My one-time hobby had turned itself into a full-fledged business, an animated television series that forced me to learn an entirely new industry for me.

Our latest home would become the second of two "Flumpstowns" to enter our lives, both successful in their own ways but neither successful in eliminating my thoughts of Rick. Try as I might, I still couldn't break free of him.

The notion that "I may actually grow old alone" worried me. Unfortunately, I couldn't figure out what to do about it. I felt stuck and it seemed that, with every effort that I made to break free, I became that much more entangled. I didn't know what to do.

"What's next for you, Evie...what?" I asked myself as I placed my laptop on the floor, switched my lamp off, and curled up in my bed. I was too tired to think anymore.

It was an answer that would begin in New York and end in London some three years later.

Chapter 21
The New Men

Dating after my loss of Rick wasn't easy. Honestly, I didn't even know where to begin. Balancing single-parenthood against the management of the television show as well as Rick's business left little time for me to squeeze in getting to know anybody. None of that prevented me from sharing a dinner here or there with some really interesting, intelligent gentlemen, mind you. The entertainment industry had no lack of eligible bachelors that's for sure. Not one, however, caught my attention profoundly enough to make it worth my time to expand the existing juggle. Until HE showed up, that is.

The man I'm referring to was a wildly successful entertainment entrepreneur turned "television network" president. He was Jewish, spoke with a thick Brooklyn accent, and was unconventionally attractive, confident, and sexy. I met him after doing an interview for an entertainment magazine. Having read that interview, he figured out how to contact me, leaving me a message with Elizabeth to ring him back. I knew exactly who he was when I read his note. My return phone call led to "dinner" the next time he was in New York.

Two weeks later, we met in-person. He had made reservations at a Turkish restaurant. I'd never eaten Turkish food before. It was the first of many times that he'd share a whole new side of life with me.

The evening sped by, his initial interest arising from my unusual personal story and the courage that I'd found to jump into unchartered waters as I had, both feet first. He jokingly told me that we shared similar stories in this regard, *which made me just as stupid as him.* I chuckled and nodded in solidarity, knowing full well what he meant.

We began dating from that moment on, me flying to Los Angeles when I could and him spending as much time in New York as possible. He mentored me, protected me from the many wolves in the industry, and introduced me to incredible people, including his family. As much as you wouldn't expect it, this man was a very down-to-earth guy. He'd never moved too far from his roots, and I liked that about him. Plus he had a knack for making incredible Chinese food from scratch, something he took with him from his years of growing up in Brooklyn.

"Sounds like quite the catch, Evie," Debra commented. "What happened?"

"I wish I could explain it, Debra. As hard as I tried, I couldn't fall in love with him. Every time he would say it to me, I just couldn't say it back."

"Really?" Debra questioned. Then in a completely different tone, she continued, "Well, you can't force love. It either *is* or it *isn't.*"

"Ain't that the truth," I answered her. "Eventually he became frustrated with me which resulted in lots of fights and then, a complete break-up. His last words to me were so cutting, I could barely breathe after he said them."

"My God, what did he say?" Debra asked.

He remarked, "What a shame it was what Rick had done to me."

"What?... What had Rick done to you?" Debra continued, really unsure of where this was going.

"To put it bluntly, Debra, and in his own words...*Rick ruined me for any other man.*"

As I said, I could barely breathe after he said it. Talk about coupling my current fears of "living the rest of my life alone" with such a callous statement. I didn't know if his response was out of hurt, self-preservation, ego or a side of him that I had missed. But it was jarring and significantly messed with my head. Admittedly a piece of me was worried that he could be right."

"I can understand that. Did you ever speak with him again?" Debra asked.

"Yes, years later. We would eventually become friends but after much time and healing. To this day, he continues to be one of my favorite people and I, his, I believe. Whenever we chat or meet-up, he asks about my four older children and then specifically Andrew, who he refers to as his *almost son.*"

"*Almost son*? Why in the world does he refer to Andrew as his *almost son*?" Debra questioned, a puzzled look washing over her face as she did.

Because I made him aware of just how life-altering his parting words were to me. Their impact changed the course of my future, I have no doubt."

"How so?" Debra asked.

"They thrust me head-first into my second marriage, I believe," I replied, "to Andrew's actual father. Somewhere inside me, I wanted to prove him wrong."

Debra nodded, "This should be good. What happened?"

"I met Andrew's father for the first time on a plane about a month after that break-up," I replied. "He was heading from London to Alpine, New Jersey, care of Newark Liberty International Airport.

The kids and I had been living in Alpine now for about a year, exchanging our previous address for one that offered a fresh beginning and an equally good school system. The kids had not wanted to move, but I thought that it was time for me to consider my own needs too. Living in Rick's and my home for the many years following his death had been extremely hard on me but I continued to do so for the sake of the children and the consistency and stability it provided them.

Now that they were getting older however I could no longer ignore my desire to move. Every room held a reminder of the wonderful times that Rick and I had shared, all of which were gone. Moments when we danced together in the living room after we put the kids to bed. The back deck where we held lavish parties complete with fully-dressed string quartets. The bedroom where we made love, not to mention found out that I was unexpectedly pregnant with Grace. Surprise!

As I sat on the floor barely able to move, Rick fished through my pajama drawer for a pregnancy test and handed it to me without saying a word. Minutes later, we'd find out that baby number four was around the corner. Rick couldn't have been more thrilled, having always said that he wanted six. He used Estelle as his excuse, but I knew otherwise.

"Six?" Debra mouthed. "Three more and you could have had a baseball team."

"I know," I replied. "But I was on board with it too."

"So you were both out of your minds," Debra replied. "Good to know. I won't write that down."

"Better you don't," I agreed. "Truthfully, knowing that I would never have another one of Rick's children was extremely tough for me to cope with after Rick died. I know that sounds stupid, Debra, but it's just how I felt."

"No judgment here," Debra responded. "I get the 'kid' thing. You already know that about me."

I nodded. "Sorry to have switched off-topic. As I was saying... then there was his workshop," I continued. "The one I surprised him with."

"Seriously?" Debra responded.

"Yup. I had it built while he was on a business trip out of town. I could still remember his face when he returned. He was astonished and thrilled all at the same time. His first project was a hammock stand, which he made for me as a "thank you." He told me that we would lay on it together while watching the kids play on the swing set in the backyard."

Unfortunately, those plans didn't quite work out as expected. Instead, they landed me in the hospital on Rosh Hashanah with a concussion, Rick alongside incessantly apologizing for his faulty work.

The stand had snapped in half when Rick went to join me in the hammock that day, one side launching into the air and knocking me out cold when it came back down. Thankfully, Estelle and Saul were able to pick up the kids in a hurry following the entire episode. Looking back now, it was funny, not unlike so many other moments Rick and I shared. But I couldn't continue to relive those memories so readily and that house was making me do it. I needed to move.

So we found a lovely home with lots of property less than thirty minutes away from Estelle and Saul, and we moved in. Thankfully, our nanny Alicia could continue with us despite the additional time it took for her to drive to our new place.

I hadn't expected to return so soon from my trip, but Alicia emailed me while I was away that there was a special pumpkin-carving event for Grace at school at the end of the week. Grace really wanted me to be there. So I switched flights and took whatever seat I could get on the plane.

I was placed next to a very handsome stranger seated in business class. He was much older than me, distinguished, with salt and pepper hair, dark eyes, and the kind of simplistic European style that I came to love from my many travels abroad. My guess was that he was not new to sitting in the seat that he did, and it turned out that my assumption was correct. I would find out later in our conversation that he was flying back to the states to celebrate one of his nephews' birthdays. Having never been married, with no kids of his own, he'd become extremely close with his brother's children over the years. He made the trip frequently, and his work allowed him to do so.

"Nice company," I said to the man I'd come to know as Colin Hadleigh.

"They get their money's worth," Colin answered with a smirk.

By the end of the flight, we had exchanged numbers. I was drawn to him and found him immensely attractive, not unlike that which I felt when I first met Rick. A tremendous amount of guilt went along with those feelings but I tried to push it aside, convincing myself that I needed to begin to "move on" or live out that reality of "growing old alone." I am certain the impact of my ex-boyfriend's comment played a role in how I was feeling too. Needless to say, we went on our first of many dates a few days later.

There was no doubt that the time that Colin and I spent together over the next eight months was a lot of fun and provided worthwhile insight into each other's lives. Colin had grown up in Manchester, England. The youngest of two children, he seemed to have lived a charmed life complete with loving parents, financial stability, and an Oxford degree.

He'd eventually go on to excel in international sales, which resulted in his becoming a rock star of sorts in his field and ultimately the senior vice president of a large consumer products firm in London. He traveled the world regularly, citing it as the reason that he had never married. "My single regret," he told me. Music to my ears, I was immediately taken with his obvious love for family and, eventually, with him...the extent of which I would learn only *after* we were married."

"So, it was good then? Or wasn't it? I'm confused," Debra remarked, seemingly holding her breath awaiting my answer.

"It wasn't good at all," I replied. The memories came flooding back.

"What happened?" Debra asked, hoping to hear the entire tale with little left out. A second thought crept in, admonishing her for being too nosey. She swept it aside and continued to listen.

Part of me wished that I could tell her the entire story, every detail of what had occurred between me and Colin. Truthfully, I'd wished I'd understood it all myself. I didn't, though, even now. As such, I decided to respond to Debra's question vaguely. "Let's just say, the entire affair wasn't pretty."

"What began as a whirlwind courtship, ended in anything but. I don't blame him entirely. I blame myself too. I wasn't in the right frame of mind to have a serious relationship at all, let alone one with an international jet-setting type. I was still figuring myself out, which left me little space to figure out how wrong Colin and I had been for each other until it was much too late."

"Sounds like there is more to the story than you are letting on, Evie," Debra replied.

"There is," I answered her. "But honestly, none of that truly matters. At the end of the day, the people I love more than anything else in the world, my kids, got hurt...again. They got hurt because of me."

Coping with that reality was harder than going through the actual divorce. My job was to protect my children, not put them into harm's way for a second time. "And what did I do? I put them into harm's way. I failed miserably and that impact was hard on all of us."

"The loss of their father, Evie, wasn't your fault. You can't blame yourself for the hurt that they had to deal with as a result of his death," said Debra.

"True," I replied, "but that doesn't make the notion that I threw a whole lot more unnecessary pain on top of them too, any easier." I sighed deeply. It was a regret I wasn't quite sure I'd ever get past, second only to my failed promise to Rick.

"I understand that, Evie, but you are not being fair to yourself," remarked Debra. "Yours was a mistake many women have made. You're not alone in that." Taking a breath, Debra would sternly continue, "Besides look at what...or should I say "whom"... it brought forth." Debra pointed again at the photo of Andrew.

"He's adorable."

"Yes, he is," I replied. "Our little silver lining in all of this for certain." I could feel a bright smile wash over my face in an instant. "He is so loved by his brother and sisters, they have designated him an honorary Remington."

"Does he see his dad at all?" Debra asked.

"Yes," I replied. "Regularly now. The transition and communication were a bit tough during the initial year of our divorce, but it got a whole lot better after that."

"Good," Debra replied. "Where does Colin live today?" she continued with her questioning.

"He's back in London. He sees Andrew every few weeks. After things calmed down between us, Colin and I both decided that it would be better for Andrew if we maintained a working relationship. *The worst was over and time heals all wounds* or so they say. In any event, that's what we do. Everyone is the better for it, including my four older children who realize the importance of Colin in Andrew's life. Having grown up without a father, themselves, they did not want a similar fate to befall Andrew too."

"Smart kids. Smart mama," Debra remarked.

Like Rick used to always remind me, "Figure out what you need to do to achieve the best of all possible outcomes, then do that." It was one of the first lessons that man ever taught me in business and I daresay, it has been one of the most valuable. And now the kids know it too.

"Evie, what you went through wasn't *business*. It was *personal* and highly emotional. Where were Estelle and Saul in all of this?"

"Right by my side every step of the way," I replied.

"Boy, your in-laws are gems," Debra answered.

"Without a doubt," I uttered, thinking back upon the many nights that I spent crying on Estelle's shoulder. She had been so patient with me. Saul too, although he seemed less forgiving of Colin's role in the entire debacle.

"Makes sense," Debra replied, then continued, "What about Baron? Do you and the kids still have a relationship with him? Did he come to your aid too?"

"Baron had been sick for a while following Rick's death. He died two years later. The IRS and attorneys' fees took most of his estate leaving very little for Rick's brothers and sisters to divide between them. It was quite sad."

"What a shame. Another story that seems quite common when a lot of money is involved. Well, at least you came out of the divorce alright."

"In the end, I did. That's true. But I don't like making mistakes. I felt broken for a while following my split with Colin. I actually thought that I was headed for a legitimate nervous breakdown."

"You did?" Debra questioned.

"Yes," I replied. "In the end, what held me together was a life-changing conversation that I would have with my long-time friend and financial advisor, Richard Weinstein. This conversation would lead me to a series of serious decisions resulting in the sale of my businesses, our move to Connecticut, and extended time off."

"Did these decisions also help you move past Rick?" Debra asked.

"Nope but they would lead me to the person who could a few years after that."

"Really?" Debra squealed. "Mind sharing?" conscious of how she might be coming across once again.

"I will," I said. "But you need to understand how this person was brought into my life before you can fully grasp the rest."

"Then keep talking, dear," Debra replied. "I'm not leavin' till the bitter end."

"That makes two of us," I smiled, "the running theme of my life, no doubt."

"I agree with that," Debra replied.

Looking at the last cookie on the plate, I refrained from sliding it onto my own. Debra probably had the same thought on her mind. *Better she has it than me*, I decided. Then once again, I began to speak, thinking back to the breaking-point that I had reached and all that had happened since. If my story hadn't already surprised my new friend, and I think it had, the rest would without question.

Chapter 22

The Crash

Phoning Richard a few days after my divorce was finalized, I could barely stop crying. It muffled my routine greeting. I felt worn out...more than I'd ever felt before. Not only had the stress over the years caught up with me but so had my grief over Rick's death. I had never truly allowed myself to feel the depth of my loss nor the hurt that went along with being "his widow." I avoided both, vehemently. I began to collapse under the strain, moving between states of depression and rage.

The final straw came when I picked up a kitchen chair and hurled it against the cabinets across the room, my response to two of the children arguing. My extreme reaction scared me as much as it did the kids. Calling Richard seemed to be the best alternative I could think of given my loss of control.

I had met Richard Weinstein through Jack Litwin, my attorney. Jack had taken care of establishing the trust for Rick's and my children. He swore by Richard and shared a great deal with me about him prior to putting me in touch. This included how

Richard had launched his own foundation to help fund a new children's hospital in Israel. I liked the idea as well as the understanding that he had a fondness for kids, given his job would be to care for the wealth of my own.

Richard was a perfect match, I decided. The one caveat in our relationship would be that, unlike everyone else who called Richard "Rick," I never would. It just wasn't a name I could easily say. Richard agreed, sensitive to my needs.

In time, he would become more than a wealth manager to me. He'd become a confidant and friend, whose insight and advice I greatly respected—a right-hand man of sorts. As such, it was only natural that I'd call him when I felt like I was falling apart.

"Evie," Richard inquired, recognizing my voice amongst the tearful stuttering. "What's wrong?"

"Richard," I answered him. "I don't know how much more that I can take. I feel like I'm having a nervous breakdown. I'm so exhausted that I can't even think. I can't do this anymore?"

"Do what, Evie?" Richard replied calmly.

"This!" I cried. "This constant juggling. These continuous reminders of Rick. I want them to go away. I can't run these companies any longer. I don't want to. Mine or his but especially *his*. It was his dream…and my dream with him…but that dream is over, and this part of my life has to be over too."

"So," Richard responded. "What you are saying to me is that *after more years than anyone could have ever expected of you…you finally hit the wall.* I was wondering when this was going to happen."

I sniffled and remained silent, absorbed and befuddled by Richard's words.

"Evie, take a few days off with the kids at the cottage and rest.

Then come into my office Monday afternoon and let's work all of this out. You don't have to work anymore, Evie. What you do with your life going forward is up to you, but that part is done if you want it to be. You are fine and so are the kids."

With a big sigh, I thanked Richard then disconnected my cell phone for the rest of the weekend. As soon as the kids returned from school that day, we took off for the cottage.

I remember sleeping a great deal that weekend—sleeping, watching rom coms, and writing in my journal. It was one of the most relaxing and peaceful times we had ever had at the cottage.

I was reminded of the solace I had found on the porch swing that hung from the back of the house that Rick and I shared. While he slept, I'd leave our bed, heat up a cup of tea, and enjoy the still-ness and beauty of the night sky. I remember during one of those times, Rachel had decided to sleep over. She joined me on the porch swing that evening, a nice change.

We shared a very honest conversation, which included many comforting words, lots of memories and what could only be de-scribed as "permission to sleep with another man" if I needed to. Rachel realized just how long it had been for me and Rick. She knew what I had been going through and how lonely I must feel. She wanted me to know, from one woman to another, that she would understand it if I made that choice. I never did, never want-ing to desecrate what Rick and I shared but I appreciated Rachel more than ever that day. I had not thought about that moment again until this weekend.

When Monday afternoon eventually rolled around, I was ready to change my life. And with Richard's help and support, I did... completely.

Over the next year, I would sell Rick's company to some of

his original employees. I accepted an offer for "The Flumps" from a Canadian competitor and sold that too. And I'd rent my Alpine address, allowing me to purchase a full-time residence in Connecticut while keeping the cottage as well.

The new home, a classic farmhouse surrounded by stone walls, was located on Cardinal's Way. I almost dropped dead when I heard the name of the street. The realtor told me that the original builder had named it this as he noticed an extraordinary number of cardinals flying about when building the home. *More irony*, I thought as we entered the long, private road leading to the driveway.

Not unexpectedly, the home spoke to me from the moment I saw it. It had been sitting empty for some time and the bank, who owned it, was more than happy to give it away. I was equally as happy to take it. Looking out over the forest of which the front porch faced, I noticed a bright red, robust cardinal sitting astutely on one of the highest branches of a lilac tree.

"I can do this," I said to myself. "I need to do this," I continued, deciding that my cardinal sighting was yet another good omen. I phoned Richard on the spot. He loved the idea and loved the price even more. We purchased the property quickly.

"It sounds like it was *meant to be*," said Debra. "Definitely so."

"I think so too," I responded, then continued. "I remember the very day we moved in. As the moving company pulled heavy boxes from the front porch, dividing them among the many rooms, the last box that remained was marked with Rick's name. It was filled with some of Rick's prized possessions. I was doling them out to the children over time. I noticed the box sitting by itself when I walked outside for a quick breath of fresh air. Perched on top was that bright red, robust cardinal that I previously mentioned.

He sat completely still as if he was inspecting me as well as what I was doing. I stared back at him studying every detail of his gorgeous coloring. I thought, *Well, if you are actually Rick in disguise, you've gained weight and have a new coat too.* I burst out laughing, thinking how crazy I must sound. Walking closer, the cardinal flew back to his branch leaving me to retrieve the box and take it inside.

I spent much of the next year of my life in restoration mode, complete with painting, furnishing, and gardening, accompanied by constant pleas to my handyman for immediate assistance. This gentleman seemed to come with the house, and when the realtor gave me his name at the closing, I wasn't surprised to learn it–Rick Maynard.

Not unlike Richard Weinstein and now Rick Maynard, there would be many Rick's throughout the children's and my lives ready to help whenever the need called, including a kind police officer who saved Victoria from a frightening car accident during her first year as a driver. The children and I began to jest that their father remained busy arranging for multiple stand-ins in his place. Somewhere in our joking however I always wondered if that was true.

When the house finally came together, it was magnificent. The exterior included a stone fire pit in the backyard, Bocce and horse-shoe courts, an enormous rose garden, a small barn, wrought iron gates, trees as far as the eye could see, and a lemonade porch to die for. The interior held five bedrooms, three bathrooms, a pool table, French doors, a flagstone fireplace, and an open layout. The kitch-en stood in the center of it all. I called it my "Writers House" as the many windows and magnificent views would inspire any writer to put "pen to paper" even a novice writer like me.

Quite paradoxically, as I went about putting our new home together, it did the same for me. I felt safe in my new surroundings, invigorated by the switch to a more laid-back lifestyle, and fortunate to be able to make many new friends while keeping hold of important old ones. The kids seemed to adjust well too. The only downside was the distance that our move imposed upon our regular visits with Estelle and Saul, but we did our best to work around this and saw them as much as possible.

The truth was, life was moving ahead, and we all needed to contend with many transitions. Our new home was only one of them. Michael was now in college, and Victoria was following closely behind. The years were speeding up for the younger three too. Changes were inevitable. That didn't make the notion of being so far away from their grandchildren any easier for Estelle or Saul. It just made it a bit more understandable. The inevitability of time was showing itself as was the realization of how long it had now been since Rick had actually passed away.

Trapped by a ghost, first, and a failed marriage, second, the combination unnerved me. It was reflected in my sparse personal life. Soon, I would no longer be able to hide behind the kids or the home I was putting together. I knew this. I would need something else to keep me occupied.

I began to concentrate on an entirely new door that opened to me through writing. The "Writer's House" that I had unexpectedly found and appropriately named would soon become my *writer's house*—with me, no longer a novice but a professional author and blogger.

The newfound "love in my life"—writing—arrived to me through an unusual twist of fate. I had decided to write an op-ed, directing it towards a young actress who had recently lost her husband in a boating accident. As the world mourned for her and her children, I thought that I might help by sharing some of the wisdom that I had collected from my own experience. I submitted it to a news site, never really expecting it to reach her. They published it.

The young actress would go on to read it and publicly thank me for my words. I'd become a recognized name overnight, with numerous publishing deals to consider. It seemed that many widows needed my advice. So I began writing and eventually speaking.

With the support of thousands of widows and mothers, I decided to launch my own blog. I called it "All's Well." I wanted the title to be uplifting.

"Great name," Debra stated, as she returned to rubbing her foot for a second time.

"Debra," I remarked. "Can I get you more ice?"

"That would be wonderful, dear. Thank you," she replied.

I rose from my chair, filled a clean bag with a few cubes, knotted it, then wrapped it up in a towel and handed it to her. "By the way," I said as she took the ice pack from my grasp, "you might want to call your ride as it won't be too much longer until you are up to speed on everything."

"Ok," she replied, grabbing her cell phone and swiftly texting a message to the person who had previously dropped her off. Once done, she turned her attention back to me and our discussion about my blog. "So what kind of information do you share exactly?" she continued.

"All types of things," I replied. "I even interview celebrities."

I thought about the many interesting names who I had met through the site. They seemed surreal. But then again, I pitched every request knowing that I had already been through hell and back again. Receiving "No" for an answer seemed trivial by comparison. It won me lots of "Yeses."

"Real celebrities?" questioned Debra.

"Yes, real celebrities."

"You gotta be kidding me?" Debra cried. "Like who?"

"You won't believe me if I tell you," I replied. "But they are all listed on the blog. You will need to find out *who* on your own." I wanted to surprise Debra, holding out to provide a proper crescendo. "I've truly met some incredible people eager to help others through their own personal stories. Before I knew it, "All's Well" had millions of followers and a backlist of popular interviews."

"That's amazing," Debra remarked. "Is that what you do now?"

"It is," I said.

"Talk about turning lemons into lemonade," Debra stated.

"I never did like lemons," I smartly retorted.

"No, you sure didn't," Debra said.

"You know what else I didn't like?" I continued.

"What?" Debra replied, still stunned by the notion that I spoke to celebrities on a regular basis.

"I didn't like seeing my daughter Grace agonize over the sour reality of never really knowing Rick, which would be something that would begin to haunt her more and more as she grew into adulthood."

"Really, now?" Debra replied. "That makes complete sense though, doesn't it?"

"I know, but it was hard for me to watch...really hard," I replied.

"Did she go to see a therapist about it?" Debra asked.

"In a way," I answered. "But not of the living kind."

"What?" Debra remarked. "What in heaven do you mean?"

"Exactly," I replied. "You hit the nail right on the head, Debra, without even knowing it."

"I'll be hittin' something else if you don't let me in on what you are speaking about pretty soon," she replied, jokingly.

"Calm down, Debra," I answered. "I'm getting there."

Just then Debra's cell phone vibrated, alerting her to the amount of time that she had left between now and the moment her ride would be in the driveway to pick her up. "Evie, he will be here in forty minutes. He's caught in traffic."

"Sounds about right," I replied. "It will allow us just enough time to finish."

"Terrific," Debra cried. "Now, might we get back to where we left off as I have no idea what you are talking about?"

"Absolutely," I said. "Mind you though, I didn't either until it happened to me. Or might I say, who?"

"Who?" Debra repeated. "Who? Who? And don't mock me that I sound like an owl."

"I won't, although you do."

"Then who?" Debra continued.

"Sebastian."

"Sebastian? Who the heck is Sebastian?" Debra cried.

"I'm getting to that part," I answered, leading me to dive into the tale resulting in my meeting of Sebastian—a man whose arrival into mine and the children's lives would forever change our world and all perceptions regarding life, death and particularly Rick.

The word "real" was about to get muddied.

Chapter 23
The Revelation

It was one of those unusual mornings when everything was running like clockwork. Andrew had dressed for school without so much as a single reminder. Breakfast had also been a breeze. Then the car. Before I knew it, Andrew was inside his classroom and settled himself at the science table where a basket of colorful leaves sat.

"See you later, Andrew," I called to him as I briskly scooted out the door. I had to get back to the house as I was scheduled to interview one of the most popular television personalities currently. He was a psychic medium that seemed to be everywhere these days.

Thomas James was the "it" guy when it came to connecting the "living" with those who had "crossed over." He had his own show, line of merchandise, and top tier clientele. I had landed the interview after doing a favor for his public relations agent regarding a lesser-known client. Thomas James was my "thank you" in return. I couldn't wait to speak with him. It was a pretty sweet "get." My readers would also think so.

I loved the work that I was doing. It was fulfilling and made me realize the necessity of "purpose" in one's life. This morning's interview was no exception. Thomas James had a *purpose*. Despite my continued skepticism that communicating with the dead was truly possible, I knew he and others *believed. Maybe he could convince me once and for all,* I thought. No doubt, there was a deep-seated hope that he could...that he'd feel Rick's presence through the phone and tell me so.

"How much peace would I receive knowing that Rick was still around and I wasn't crazy?" I said to myself. Even so, I refused to become preoccupied with the idea. I decided that I wouldn't request a personal reading during the interview when all that Thomas James had planned to do was to speak about his upcoming tour. *That would be tacky and hardly professional.*

"Who knows," I said as I reviewed my notes and retrieved his cell phone number from the email his press agent had provided.

Twenty minutes later, we were done. Not one word about Rick had been mentioned. *You see,* I thought to myself. *You've spent a lifetime misconstruing your tie to Rick as something more, when it's been nothing but your way of hanging on to a past you really don't want to give up.*

I couldn't help but berate myself for my years of foolishness. At the same time, the small voice inside me refused to agree. "You've been right all along, and you needn't get Thomas James' confirmation to prove it."

I sat for a minute, reviewing my scribble from the interview and thinking further. There was one other part of this whole thing that I needed to contend with. It centered upon a recent conversation with Grace—the focus of which was two-fold. It included her "occasional seeing of Rick while growing up," similar to me, as well as "her insatiable need to know more about him."

She was having an emotional crisis, and I couldn't figure out how to help her. Glimpses of the man whose eyes she shared, offered by old DVDs and lengthy conversations, didn't seem to be enough. She needed more. I didn't know how to give that to her. Grace was the only child who couldn't retrieve a single memory of her father. She had been too young when everything happened. And even though, in some ways that reality was a blessing, in others, it was a curse.

"It was ironic that the one child who couldn't remember a thing about him was the same child who believed that she could feel his presence," I said to Debra.

"It certainly is," she replied. "Maybe that says something?'

Again, I shook my head.

Thinking further on the matter, I wrote up Thomas James' interview then earmarked it for next month's issue. Once done, I called a few of the bloggers that blogged for me and chatted with them about the stories they were writing as well as a few additional odds and ends that seemed to always go along with maintaining a rolling editorial calendar. A bunch of workaholics, everyone was keeping pace like usual. It was very rare that I ever needed to run any of them down for a promised piece.

As the last of my phone calls was to a woman named Jo, a blogger who also happened to be a good friend, our conversation transitioned effortlessly. She had known that I was interviewing Thomas James that morning and she could not wait to hear what he and I had spoken about, which easily opened the door to discussing my problem with Grace.

"Did you really think that he was going to detect Rick from over the phone?" Jo asked.

"I don't know," I replied. "How do I know what these types of individuals can do?"

"Maybe you should call him back and ask him for a favor, give you a reading *on him*? Use it as part of the interview you are writing," Jo continued.

"Nah," I replied. "I already thought of that and nixed the idea. I'd feel foolish. Besides, I'd hate to piss the guy off or his public relations firm. You know how they can be when they have a hot commodity on their hands. I wouldn't want to chance it."

"I understand. You're right," Jo said.

"Any other thoughts?"

"Not this second but let me talk to Scott. You never know what he will suggest."

Scott was Jo's husband. A great guy, he worked as a teacher a few towns over from where they lived. He loved his job even though the pay was less than livable. That was the reason Jo had reached out to me when she learned that I had launched "All's Well."

As writing was her passion too, she thought doing so regularly for me would add to the family income and kill two birds with one stone. I was glad to have her help as I needed another reliable pair of hands at the time to manage the rapidly increasing workload.

"Thanks, Jo," I said.

"No problem," Jo replied. "I'll let you know if he comes up with anything."

"Sounds good," I answered. As I hung up the phone, I couldn't help but think to myself how nuts this all sounded but where my child was involved, I'd do anything to help. "The cardinal rule of parenting," I said to myself as I peered out the window in search of that bird. He was nowhere to be found.

He later returned. I spotted him while watching Andrew hop off the bus and run to the front door of our home. Andrew rushed inside to have a snack and grab his baseball glove. He had practice that afternoon and didn't want to be late. An active child, more so than the four that preceded him, I could barely keep up with every sport Andrew wanted to play.

"Hi Andrew," I said, kissing him on the top of the head. "You have fifteen minutes to eat your pizza, then it's out the door."

"I know, Mom," Andrew shouted. "Remember, practice is longer tonight as we have a game on Saturday."

"I remember," I replied. "Let me just run upstairs and grab a sweatshirt." I always got cold sitting and watching these practices. It didn't seem to matter what season it was. Today was already chilly, however. And knowing that I'd kick myself if I forgot, I wanted to get one before it slipped my mind among the many other things occupying it.

"Can you grab my practice jersey while you're up there?" Andrew asked.

"Sure thing," I replied.

Some thirty minutes later, I was sitting in a camping chair watching Andrew play. It was the perfect chair to do so, comfortable and nowhere near a campsite. I had been given the chair as a birthday gift by my older kids years back. They loved the idea of camping. I didn't. I appreciated the gift anyway, especially now that Andrew was always practicing something.

Sipping my coffee, I heard my phone ring. It was Jo again I realized, a photo of her and Scott popping up on my screen.

"Hi Jo," I answered.

"Hi back," she replied. "I have something really interesting to tell you."

"Yes," I said, in a curious tone. "What is it?"

"Well," she said. "Scott just got home, and I mentioned to him what you and I had discussed about Grace. He said something really unexpected...an unusual suggestion of sorts."

"He did?" I questioned.

"Yes, he did," she replied. "Scott said that he knows a guy who works at another school. He seems to be able to communicate with the dead because he, himself, died before. There is some sorta correlation. He doesn't know what. In the end, however, it gave him the ability to communicate with those who have passed on."

"Are you kidding me?" I squealed, marveling at how little we, humans, actually realize about life and death.

"I'm not," she replied. "He told Scott that he has helped many people contact their loved ones from the other side.

Scott says that he is sure that this man would be happy to help Grace and you but that you must be aware of one term before he contacts him."

"What's that?" I asked anxiously.

"This guy doesn't want to lose his job. He lives a normal life with a wife and kids. So you can't tell anyone about what he can do unless he gives you his permission beforehand. Scott already has it, but you need to agree."

"I agree. I agree," I answered.

"Then I will have Scott give him your number," Jo replied.

"Thanks so much, Jo," I said. "And thank Scott for me too."

"I will. He's happy to help."

"One last thing," I asked prior to Jo hanging up. "How much does this guy charge?" Thomas James charged a bundle so I was expecting a large figure to be thrown my way.

"He charges fifty dollars for gas. It's up to you if you want to tip him on top. People usually do. He will stay for as long as you want. He told Scott that he doesn't do this for money. He just likes to help people."

"Wow," I said. "Isn't that something?"

"Apparently...and so is "he" according to Scott," said Jo. "Let me know how it goes after you speak with him."

"I will. Thanks again, Jo," I replied.

"Don't mention it. You'd do the same for me." With that, Jo hung up, leaving me to watch the rest of Andrew's practice while considering all of the possibilities that lie ahead for Grace, me and the rest of the family.

Would meeting this gentleman bring peace-of-mind or more heart-ache? I thought. I wasn't quite sure, but I knew that I had to find out...if not for Grace, my own curiosity and the gnawing questions that held me stagnant for far too long. It would all be worth it if I could talk with Rick just one last time. I needed this. I needed it more than I realized.

Chapter 24
The Call

It was around ten that evening when I received the phone call I'd been waiting for. My heart jumped when I heard the first ring… then the second. I pounced before the third could sound.

"Hello," I said.

"Hi. My name is Sebastian Somerville. I'm looking for Evie Remington."

"I'm Evie," I replied nervously.

"Evie, Scott Monty gave me your number. He said that you and your daughter could use my help."

"Yes, I believe we could," I replied. "When might you be available to meet?"

"How about a week from this Saturday," Sebastian answered. "I'm sorry it can't be sooner but I'm scheduled to go away with my family this weekend and between work and coaching, it's the best I can do."

"No worries," I replied. "I understand."

"Thanks," Sebastian said. "If you could do me the favor of texting me your address in the meantime, I'd appreciate it. Would twelve o'clock work for you?"

"Twelve would work perfectly," I responded.

"Just one last thing," Sebastian continued. "How many people will be joining us?"

Thinking quickly, I said, "Me and all three of my daughters… if that's alright?"

"It's up to you. I will stay for as long as you'd like. Also, I must tell you that sometimes spirits begin coming through to me while I'm driving over to a session...especially if they are particularly strong. If that happens, I will make sure to tell you about it when I arrive."

"Ok," I replied, struck by the life this guy must lead. "Must be something to be him," I thought to myself as I considered my limited experience with the great beyond.

"Terrific. I am looking forward to meeting all of you," Sebastian said and hung up the phone.

No sooner did I follow suit when my mind began to race with excitement and fear. Telling the girls became my priority. "How to?" my concern. *They might just think I'm bonkers,* I decided. *Finally over-the-edge, in fact, after years of missing their dad.* There was only one way to find out.

I decided to tell them in the morning. In the meantime, I turned on the television to help me declutter my mind. I knew the period between now and meeting Sebastian in-person would be very busy. I was grateful for this. I needed more than a hot minute to wrap my head around the possibility of speaking with Rick. The idea of revisiting moments in our past together shook me. I needed to understand a few things. I also needed his forgiveness for the promise that I had broken. I knew I'd never be able to move forward without it or have another relationship.

Meeting Sebastian would afford me the closure that I'd been seeking. It would provide me the opportunity to share my appreciation with Rick for his love as well as the prints that he'd left all over my life, then and ever since. No doubt, the woman that I had become was partly due to him. My future however was up to me. Still consumed by the yearning of wanting to be "in love" again, I needed to lay Rick's and my relationship to rest. I shuddered at the idea but I also knew that it was inevitable.

Scrolling through the television guide, I began to think about an interview that I was doing the following day. I learned about this woman through a morning news program. She was the head of a large nonprofit whose mission was to help place foster children in suitable homes. Having spent a great deal of time researching how the foster care system worked, it became clear to me that more needed to be done. The loss of my mother when I was young made me even more sympathetic to these kids.

So I decided to lend a hand in hopes of unearthing additional families. There just weren't enough to go around. My becoming part of the solution however wasn't helping me wind down for the night. I would eventually force myself to sleep the best that I could. It wasn't perfect but it would do.

Chapter 25
The Reckoning

The girls were scattered throughout the house when Sebastian arrived. There was no question of Grace's enthusiasm about the opportunity to communicate with her dad. Victoria and Joyce, however, seemed to be a bit more skeptical. That said, they were still interested in participating.

"Evie," Sebastian said as I opened the door. "I'm Sebastian, although you can call me Bas."

"Hi Bas," I replied. "Thanks so much for coming."

"My pleasure," Bas answered. Walking into the foyer, he questioned where the most comfortable place would be in our home to hold the session. I suggested the family room and he followed me in.

"Girls," I called. "Sebastian is here."

Each of them arrived in the room at their own pace. As they did, I could feel their nervousness grow. Bas could evidently feel it too, and he did everything that he could to put the girls' minds at ease, beginning with trading names as he had done with me.

"By the way," he said. "I had a number of spirits come to me on my way over here today. Seems like a lot of people want to talk with you guys."

Amazed and befuddled by this, I couldn't imagine who among our deceased relatives would be so eager to chat with us besides Rick, my mother...and maybe Great-Grandpa Tom. "We come from a history of strong personalities," I joked.

"I'm not surprised." Bas smiled then took the chair directly opposite the couch where the girls sat. Positioning myself closest to Grace, I surveyed each of my daughter's expressions in hopes that they would indicate to me who might want to go first. Not one of them made a peep, leaving Bas to take the floor. Our apprehension was growing.

"How is everyone feeling about this?" he asked, focusing on each of the girls then me to see if he could lighten the mood.

Victoria let out an anxious laugh, then replied, "Honestly, I don't know what to feel. I'm sorta caught somewhere between excited and scared."

Bas responded in a gentle tone, "What do you think there is to be scared about? I'm sorry. I forgot your name."

"Victoria," she said.

"Victoria," he repeated. "What's making you nervous?"

"I really don't know," Victoria replied. "I just don't know what to expect."

"That's pretty usual," Bas responded. "Why don't you let me tell you and then we can go from there. Sound good?"

"Sounds good," she answered as the rest of us nodded in unison.

Bas began. "The first thing I will do is tell you how I came by my abilities so that you understand a bit more about me. I will then explain how the process will go. After that, we can let the rest just flow. The one thing that I ask in all of this is that I have your solemn word that you will keep what happens here today secret. I have a life to protect, alongside a family. Many people don't understand what I do. They feel threatened by it. I don't want to risk my job because of my abilities or my desire to help you. Do you understand?"

"We understand," I replied.

"Great," he said. "Also you need to know that spirits are overjoyed when they have the opportunity to communicate with their loved ones. So don't be surprised if a lot of them come forward at once or that they all want to speak at the same time. That said, if you want to talk with one over the other, just let me know. I will ask the others to step aside and allow the spirit you want to converse with to remain. Your mom indicated that you are particularly interested in talking with your father. Is that right?"

Grace answered quickly, "Yes."

"Well, I know he is eager to talk with you too. He said so in the car on the way over here and again, just as I sat down now. He's currently in the room, along with many others." Bas paused, then continued. "But let's back up so that you understand how all of this began for me. I wasn't always aware of my abilities. I figured it out briefly as a child and then again after I died."

Bas would go on to share a few stories about himself as a young boy. There were plenty of times when his parents would find him holding lengthy conversations with no one else in sight. Having grown up in a very religious household, Bas's psychic medium abilities were dismissed as child's play. Understanding his parents' traditional beliefs and not wanting to disappoint them in any way,

Bas would eventually bury his otherworldly talents altogether.

Years later, when Bas was married and in his mid-thirties, an unexpected event occurred that would return them to him. Bas endured a sudden heart attack and died. It happened quickly. Out for a run, Bas's chest began to pound. Pain immediately shot through his arm. He fell to his knees and before long, his face crashed onto the sidewalk. The next thing Bas remembered, he was exiting his body and ascending towards a white light.

The peacefulness that embraced him as he continued to be drawn nearer could barely be described. Bas became caught up in it, welcoming the comfort he felt as he floated higher. He could see the image of his body lying on the ground. There was a crowd of people that surrounded it now—all panicked and not knowing what to do. But Bas no longer cared. He wanted to stay in the white light forever.

As he floated further upward, Bas began to recognize the outline of a face. It was his grandfather. The joy that Bas felt in seeing him again brought a happiness and serenity that he had not experienced in a very long time. The stress of everyday life and the pressures of having a family seemed to occupy most of his thoughts before this inexplicable twist of fate. And although he would not have traded his wife and kids for the world, what he was experiencing now was not of "this world" and he wanted nothing more than to remain. But that wasn't to be.

Within seconds of seeing his grandfather's face, he observed his expression change. It was now one of great resistance. He expressed to Bas that it wasn't his time to die and that he needed to go back. Bas began to struggle against his grandfather's wishes. He didn't want to return to his body or his life. It wasn't up to him, however.

Suddenly, without any warning, Bas's ascension reversed course at an indescribable pace. Before he knew it, a crushing pain surged throughout his body. He could barely cope with its intensity. It was then that the paramedic cried out that he had "found a pulse."

Bas would be rushed to the local hospital thereafter. He would remain for two weeks. The emergency room physician had declared that Bas had suffered a massive heart attack, something he would now need to be treated for preventatively. Bas would suffer two more before he was released from the hospital. He would never experience another heart attack again. What he would experience however was the re-emergence of his psychic medium abilities to a degree that he couldn't recall as a child.

"Spirits were coming to me all the time, day and night. They were speaking to me about everything...everything that they wanted their loved ones to know. "

"So, you hear actual voices?" Joyce asked.

"Not in the way that you are probably thinking," Bas replied. "I feel their thoughts through *here*."

Bas motioned to an area in his chest that I recognized quite well. It had been the same place where I heard Great-Grandpa Tom's thoughts when I encountered him as a kid and those of Rick's too since his passing. I couldn't believe it. All this time I hadn't been crazy. Rick WAS communicating with me. I just refused to believe it.

No wonder I haven't been able to move on. He really has been here the entire time. I suddenly realized just how married Rick and I still were. Death hadn't parted us. He hadn't left me, keeping the promise that he had made over and over throughout the years. And I refused to let him go, keeping mine in the only way that I had left.

My entire life since losing Rick began to finally make sense. All the choices that came to be, the crossroads that I had faced, the questions that remained looming in my head since his death—even my marriage to Colin—I now understood everything. Rick had been here for all of it. No more questioning my sanity nor justifying the road that I had taken. None of it was necessary any longer. I had my answer.

What I had suspected was right. Rick's presence in my life had been very much alive and very real, beyond mere memories or hoping. Our marriage had crossed worldly boundaries. Rick had stuck around out of love for me. His promise had never been broken even when his body was. He had taken it to the grave and well-past it too.

Unaware of the amount of time that I had been consumed by my thoughts, Bas called my name twice. "Evie. Evie. Is everything alright?"

"Yes," I replied. "Sorry. I just got caught up in my own head."

"That's fine," Bas said. "So let's see. Would you like to go first or would you prefer your daughters to? There seems to be a spirit here—a woman—who desperately wants to speak with Joyce." Joyce immediately perked up.

"Well then, I'd say we should let her," I replied.

As time went on we'd speak to several family members and close friends from the other side, beginning with Joyce's grandmother, my mom. Eventually, however, we would be forced to ask everyone to step aside so that the girls and I could speak with Rick.

"Did he come through?" Debra interrupted.

"Yes, he did," I replied.

"What did he say?" Debra asked, anxiously.

"A lot," I continued. "He first spoke with Joyce and talked about a problem she had been struggling with regarding school.

Joyce was floored as she listened to Rick's sound advice with Bas's help.

Bas told us at the onset that we were to think about what we wanted to know and the spirit would speak his answer to Bas. Bas would, in turn, relay that answer. Alternately, the spirits would do the same. The latter scenario was the way the initial conversation between Joyce and Rick came about. Rick had been worried about Joyce and wanted to reassure her that all would be fine."

"What happened then?" asked Debra.

"He spoke with the other girls. He told Victoria that he'd like to see her organize her life better. She had been running around a lot lately, and he suggested to temper this a bit. Grace was another matter, altogether.

"Really?" Debra cried.

"Really," I answered.

With Grace, Rick told her that she had been right all along. He had been sitting at the foot of her bed each night. He did so hoping to bring her comfort in the only way that he could. "The ghost thing wasn't perfect," he quipped, hoping to egg a smile from her. None was forthcoming.

He would go on to apologize for not being there in the way that she had needed him to be while growing up. Grace remained quiet and let Rick's words sink in, her original enthusiasm overshadowed by her father's obvious remorse.

Ultimately, he reassured the girls that he had been keeping watch over them and would continue to do so...always. He also shared how proud he was of all of them and of how well they had done despite the loss that they had endured so early in their lives. He ended by telling them that he loved them dearly. There wasn't a dry eye in the room at that point."

"There's not one in here either," Debra commented, picking up her napkin and wiping a freshly laden tear from her lower lashes. "What did he say next? To you, I mean."

"Before Bas allowed Rick to speak to me, he asked if I still wanted the girls to remain with us as Rick and I talked? Concerned for our privacy, he wanted to make sure that I felt comfortable sharing the dialogue that was about to occur.

My momentary hesitation was followed by my approval to let them stay. I did not believe there was anything to hide and much to gain from their presence, including a depth of honesty few families ever experienced together. As Rick had done with the girls prior, he initiated our first exchange."

He said, "Evie, I have to begin by thanking you."

Bas was energetically motioning with his hands as he conveyed Rick's words to me, further emphasizing their intensity. "Thank you for doing such a great job with the children....and everything. I wish I could express to you how grateful I am for this in a better way...just know that I am. What you've done is amazing."

I sighed deeply. Tears began to well up in my eyes again. Bas broke in. "He says you have some unanswered questions you need to ask him."

I nodded in response. Bas continued.

"He wants you to know that he's aware that you have been struggling with these for some time now and that he misses seeing that beautiful smile of yours. He wants you to begin to share it again with those around you. He wants you to be happy because he is happy. He wants you to know that he wasn't at first—that he fought hard to *stay*; to keep his promise to you in the state that he had made it. It took him a very long time to accept his death and to cross over but when he finally did, he found peace. He remains very happy in the company of many loved ones."

Bas stopped for a moment, using his own thoughts to slow Rick's conversation down. Rick was speaking very quickly and Bas needed to catch up. They continued. "He told me to tell you that Pop says hello."

I nearly chuckled...then responded by asking Rick to "do the same."

"Your husband's a funny guy," Bas uttered.

"*Incorrigible* is what I used to say," recalling those moments affectionately.

Bas nodded, then continued. "Rick wants you to know that you made the right decision in forcing him to let go in the hospital. He says that he understands how hard that must have been for you, just as hard as it had been for him to 'give up' or give you the answer you needed regarding marrying again after he passed."

"He says he's very sorry for this, Evie. He just couldn't bear the idea of your being with another man at the time and that it is still hard for him. He says that he now realizes however that he can't continue to hold onto you because by doing so, he has robbed you of your beautiful smile. He doesn't want this any longer. He wants you to be happy. He's letting you go, Evie. He wants you to do the same...to ultimately find someone else to love in his place."

In the throes of convulsing sobs, I felt like a weight had, finally, been lifted—allowing me to breathe again. Every unanswered question that I had been grappling with since the day I lost Rick had been answered once and for all. It relieved me of enormous guilt, regret, and confusion. The only one that remained was whether or not I could do what Rick had now given me his blessing to do—let him go and find another.

"Evie. He says it's time, and that he has faith in you. He wants you to smile again." Bas motioned, demonstrating a wide smile while lifting his left hand and pointing to its fourth finger.

"He says that he will bring someone into your life if need be… his final act of fulfilling his promise in an entirely new way that you deserve."

The girls sat completely still—stunned by the intimate and remarkable exchange between their parents that they were witnessing. Wiping both my eyes with my palms, I mustered the smile that Rick longed to see and uttered to him in a weakened voice, "You just may have to."

It would be the last time that I would ever speak with Rick again or even feel him around. Rick would leave us that day, a changed family—more whole, more secure, and more alive than ever before. Grace was still able to sense Rick's presence but I no longer could, leaving me a bit frustrated at first. In time, however, I would realize just how ridiculous my behavior was especially considering the reason I could no longer do so. Rick was once again keeping his promise to me.

The love Rick and I shared was the rare kind of love that I could only hope our children would experience for themselves one day. But I couldn't hold onto it in the way that I'd been doing any longer. I needed to free myself as Rick had asked and refind the smile that I'd buried the day I buried Rick. The life we had known together was now, officially, *over*.

"That is the most romantic story that I have ever heard," burst out Debra. Her voice was shaking with emotion. "Did you ever invite Sebastian back again?"

"No need to," I replied. "We all moved on. Sometimes you have to know when 'enough is enough'."

"That's true," Debra agreed. "So where are you now in your opinion?"

"I'm in a very good place," I replied. "Since that point, a lot has happened."

"Another man, perhaps?" Debra prompted, hoping that my response would fulfill her every wish for yet another fascinating plot twist.

"Not quite yet," I replied. "I haven't had much luck in that department, unfortunately."

"It takes time," Debra said.

"I know. I'm just tired of kissing frogs. The last one I almost kissed was a former professional baseball player who ended up being so self-absorbed, I'm certain he could have easily carried on our entire dinner conversation without me."

"You don't say," Debra chuckled.

"I do. Having the wonderful time that he did, he asked me out again and was dumbstruck when I declined. I think I said all of ten words throughout the entire evening."

"I wish I could have been a fly on the wall for that," Debra snickered.

"Yup. I'm sorta hoping that Rick delivers me that prince as he promised." I sighed as I said it.

"Hey, you never know," Debra replied. "He's come through for you before."

"That's true," I replied. "There is one part in all of this however that I'm still grappling with. It is not something Sebastian could reveal during our session nor Rick could answer for me even if he does "come through." It is an aspect of 'moving on' that I continue to remain quite stumped by...a critical one that I hadn't thought about until after I closed the door on me and Rick."

"What's that?" Debra asked.

I responded, "Even if I meet this right guy, how do I fall as deeply in love with him without diminishing the specialness of the love and relationship that Rick and I once shared? I'm not quite sure how to do this." Having thought about it countless times since my conversation with Rick, I continue to be just as confused.

"That's easy," Debra replied. "Evie, when you meet the next man you are meant to be with, that question will answer itself. In fact, you will wonder why you were even concerned about it. And remember, you're a "different" person now, Evie, *different* than when you met Rick. Your new Mr. Right will be too."

"That's exactly what this woman said, a stranger who I recently met in the airport on my way back from California. We bumped into each other while waiting for our flights and began talking. She was heading to Arizona to buy a home near her children and grandchildren. Our stories were similar with regard to losing our husbands, the men we had long considered to be the "love of our lives." She had young kids to raise too at the time.

Years into it, she would eventually meet her second husband. "When she did," she said, "falling hopelessly in love came easy." The new person that she had become met the exact right man for her current stage of life. Both men were worlds apart in demeanor but she loved each just as deeply.

She said to me that "one needn't overshadow the other." That there would be enough distance between them to prevent this. She'd go on to explain that "it would almost feel as if I'd lived two separate lives in one lifetime, having two great loves as well, one for each."

I so appreciated her words and the fact that she had taken the seat next to me when she did. I sensed that she had been placed there purposely to help lessen my confusion on the matter. "Same with you Debra," I continued.

Rising from my seat, I walked over to Debra's chair and hugged her. She patted my shoulders as she did the same. Then returning to my chair, I remarked, "Debra, I believe you were sent to me for many reasons, including confirming what this woman had already said...a double push in the right direction."

"Could be," Debra replied. "The Lord works in mysterious ways." Then shifting conversations, Debra continued. "So tell me a bit more about life today, Evie? You mentioned that 'lots has happened'.... What does that mean?"

"It means that the kids are all thriving and so am I. My business is incredible too. I feel so fortunate to be doing what I am doing," I replied.

"Evie, you've earned it," Debra remarked.

"I know but realizing that doesn't keep me from pinching myself daily. My work is a continuous adventure, full of wonderful experiences, people, and opportunities which includes you, Debra."

"Why thank you, dear. I feel the same way about you. I had no idea our time together was going to turn out this way, but I am very glad it did. I've learned more than I need to know already and feel very confident in you."

"Thanks Debra," I replied.

"Just one more question," she continued. "With all that you have been through and such a rich and interesting career presently, do you really want to add another child to the fold? Haven't you been through enough?"

I sat quietly listening—having pondered this question in my head over and over for some time now. She was right for asking it. That said, I was not without my answer. I knew that adopting a child from foster care would have its challenges, but it was because of my ability to overcome my own that I felt completely wanting and prepared to help a foster child do the same.

"Some would say that I am crazy," I replied. "I know that Debra. But if my life has taught me one thing, it is that "love" is boundless. If I can share this with a child that may never know this otherwise, or feel it for that matter, I want to. I promise...I'm not fooling myself."

"Seems to me, you never did," Debra answered. "Ok, then. Let's get to the paperwork. There's a great deal here, and we need to complete it quickly."

"I'll grab a second pen," I replied, excited by the notion that a new little boy or girl would be joining our happy family in about six months. *How far we have come*, I thought. *How far 'I' have come.*

Chapter 26
The Conclusion

After signing the last page of the packet Debra handed to me prior, I slid the entire folder back to take with her and review.

"What's next?" I asked.

"Next includes fourteen weeks of training and the learning of everything in here," Debra replied, handing me a binder seemingly three inches thick. "When Jonah, my ride, arrives he will be bringing you an additional book. You must read it. It shares case studies of successful and unsuccessful foster families, giving you real insight and helpful tips to ensure that you, your family, and your new foster child acclimate well to each other."

"Fourteen weeks?" I repeated, immediately figuring out how that obligation would fit into my already jammed schedule.

"Yes, but the classes are only held once a week for three hours at a time. There are an additional four classes outside of that, which you must also attend. Those cover basic safety measures as well as methods of coping with psychological or physical trauma. Be aware though that you can only miss one class in the entire series.

More than that and you will not be allowed to complete the training, delaying your licensing until a future time when you can take the entire course over."

"Boy, that's strict," I remarked.

"Yes," Debra replied. "It's necessary though as there is a great deal of material you need to learn and all of it, applicable."

"I understand. I will make sure I keep those dates."

"In addition, Evie, you will need to have your chimney, well, fire alarms, and smoke detectors inspected and certified in working order. Also, if we see anything that requires reinforcing, changing or fixing around your home, you must show proof that this request is completed before we will allow any foster child to stay. Which brings me to another question," Debra stated.

"What is that?" I answered.

"Would you prefer to adopt a boy or a girl?"

I had thought about this for a while and had decided upon a boy—one who was close in age to Andrew so that they may grow up together and have things in common to share and play. "I'd prefer a boy."

"Wonderful," Debra said. "Unfortunately, boys have a harder time in the system...less likely to be chosen... so the fact that you want a boy is just great!"

"I'm glad that helps," I replied.

"It does," Debra said. "I'm assuming that you would like the little guy to be around Andrew's age? I'd recommend a year younger to keep Andrew's pecking order intact. We don't want him feeling threatened, now do we? Being the big brother will help in the transition."

"I had not thought about that, but I guess it would."

"That's why I'm here, Evie. To help think of everything as your family and the foster child navigate this new terrain together. Expect me to become your new best friend, for the short term anyway and hopefully longer," Debra said with a knowing smile plastered upon her face.

"That's news I'm happy to hear," I replied warmly.

"Perfect," Debra answered, then continued. "Besides, by the looks of it, I'm moving in. Where is that Jonah?"

"The road construction around here tends to be heavy, Debra. I'm not surprised."

Suddenly Debra and I could hear a car pull up in the driveway. Two minutes later, a tall gentleman climbed the stairs and walked towards the front door. Spotting him through the large bay window, Debra said, "Wonderful. Finally, Jonah is here. I will introduce you as you will be working closely together over the next few months too."

"Why's that?" I asked, not knowing who this Jonah was other than the person currently shuttling Debra around.

"That," Debra responded, "is because Jonah is involved in helping many of the foster children mentally and emotionally cope with leaving one family and transitioning to another. He is a very brilliant psychiatrist actually. He leads the entire mental health team dedicated to our foster care program in the state of Connecticut."

"That has to be a very challenging job," I replied, rising from the table and heading towards the door.

"It is," Debra said. She continued to remain seated, not eager to put any weight on her tender foot any earlier than required.

"Well, then...we'd better let him in," I teased as I gripped the doorknob and pulled—my eyes remaining focused on Debra all the while. Then shifting them forward as not to be rude, I opened the door.

A sudden, totally unexpected jolt overtook me. There, on the other side, stood an incredibly attractive man. I immediately fell silent, paralyzed by his disheveled good looks and warm, laid-back manner. Flowing black waves tinged with silver settled at the base of his neck, providing background to a well-kept beard and broad smile, the kind that consumes a person's entire face. Shaking me out of it, Debra called out, "I thought you were going to let him in?"

She rose from the table and decided to join me in the foyer. A bright red, robust cardinal suddenly shot out of nowhere and darted right past our new visitor's head. Jonah ducked instinctively in response. "What the heck was that?" he remarked, a bit startled by the bird's unexpected appearance.

"A cardinal. Ain't you ever seen a cardinal before? You city boys," she snickered, waving her associate in as I pushed open the screen door. Then turning towards me, Debra noticed my unusual silence. She also took note of the type of bird that had just made its presence known to all of us. Recognizing "romantic interest" when she spotted it, Debra lifted her eyebrows, hoping to establish that "what she was reading" was true.

I answered with a big grin, immediately telling her all that she needed to know.

Her lips took on a Cheshire-cat type response, then launching into the routinely formal introduction, Debra said, "Dr. Jonah Erickson, Meet Evie Remington." As his full name rolled from her tongue, I could see a second light bulb go off in Debra's head just as it had mine.

Erickson? I thought, struck by the "Rick" in Jonah's last name. Another thought abruptly emerged. It was the one that I had just discussed with Debra moments earlier, revealing Rick's promise to me that he would bring someone to my doorstep if need be.

"Was this him?" I said to myself. "Could Rick be fulfilling his final promise to me through Debra—one last selfless act of love like he said?"

Neither alone in my thinking nor certain of what to do next other than carry on as if nothing unusual was happening, I met Dr. Jonah Erickson's open hand with that of my own. Initiating a reasonable amount of congenial chit-chat alongside, I looked towards Debra for needed direction. I was a bit flustered as to how to proceed.

Debra instantly took hold of the conversation. "Jonah, I was just telling Evie about you. I told her that you two will be working closely together in making sure all goes well with the fostering and ultimate adoption of one lucky kid."

"Yes, we will," Jonah replied. "I'm looking forward to helping you, Evie, so don't you worry, Ok?"

"Ok," I replied.

"Which reminds me," Jonah said. "This is for you." He took a thick book out from under his arm and handed it to me. "More reading." His smile nearly knocked me off my feet.

Nervous laughter accompanied a witty, unrehearsed response. "Great. 'War and Peace', the foster care edition."

Observing the banter transpiring between us, Debra stepped back from interrupting.

"Oh, yes…absolutely," Dr. Jonah Erickson responded with amusement in his voice. "But then again, you knew what you were getting yourself into when you signed up for this, right Evie?" He paused then continued, "You know what they say, *Be careful what you wish for*."

"She sure does," Debra cried as I stood completely stunned by the phrase Jonah had just pulled out of the air. It had not been lost on Debra either, "How about I let you guys schedule the sessions required while I gather my things?"

As she left the room for the kitchen again, I could hear her note under her breath, "Dear God, I've never heard that old saying spoken so many times in one day."

Jonah had no idea what she was talking about, but he understood from her comment that he had just walked in on something. "Any idea what she means?" he asked.

"Not in the least," I replied, doing my best to indicate nothing at all.

Jonah suspected otherwise. The expression on his face told me so. He stood analyzing mine to somehow delineate whether or not I was telling the truth. When nothing more was forthcoming on the matter, he paused no longer.

It was the first of many such exchanges between Jonah and me. Ours was a relationship that had just begun, and as anticipated, it would progress well beyond the unique circumstances in which we had met. In time, Jonah would become much more to me. He would become my husband.

We would marry two years later, adopt a five-year-old son between us and add him to our happy home. During moments throughout our courtship, I would share with Jonah stories about Rick, including his hand in my life following his passing. Jonah just accepted these stories as truth and left it at that.

"He did me a favor," he said in response, "and for this, I am eternally grateful."

"Me too," I agreed, as I reminded myself how silly I had once been for worrying about how another man would fit into my heart without tarnishing what Rick and I had once shared. The question had answered itself as Debra and the woman in the airport had said it would.

My life with Rick seemed like a lifetime ago now. I never thought it would happen, but it was true. Today, I was deeply in love with Jonah, unable to imagine my world without him. It was a whole new chapter for both of us and I was smiling.

Hugging Jonah with all of my might, I said to myself, "As long as I live, I will still never have enough time with this man." It was a profound statement, causing me to reflect upon where I was today as well as the incredible path that had landed me here, nestled next to Jonah in complete bliss. *I wouldn't have missed a single minute of it,* I thought.

Looking up in the air, I couldn't help but mouth a silent "thank you" to Rick, wherever he happened to be. As I did, that same cardinal that nearly pummeled Jonah when we first met suddenly appeared in the kitchen window. With it, a warm sensation unexpectedly grazed my cheek.

Lifting my hand to my face, I touched it knowingly. Then as quickly as both had come, they were gone.

We'd see the cardinal again the following spring. He returned with his new family, a wife and a few babies. Jonah built a lovely birdhouse for all of them. He placed it a few feet outside of our front porch, making it easy for us to sit on our swing and watch. Rick, however, would never be back.

I often wondered if a piece of Jonah had erected that birdhouse in deference to Rick, to pay his respects to a man who he'd never met but whose path he'd undoubtedly crossed...or if he merely wanted to make me happy. I never asked him. I didn't need that answer as I already had all that I could wish for now...including comfort in the knowledge that everyone I had ever cared about and loved was finally home.

To be continued…

Author Laura J. Wellington &
Her Late Husband Dean R. Wellington